SAFE CORRIDOR

Jan Dost

Safe Corridor (Novel)

Originally published as '*Mamarr Amin*'

Translated by: Marilyn Booth

Bait Alghsham DarArab International Translation Prize 2024

Winner of Translators' Category

60 Blakes Quay
Gas Works Road
RG1 3EN
Reading, United Kingdom
info@dararab.co.uk
www.dararab.co.uk

First Edition 2025
ISBN 978-1-78871-112-8

@DarArabUK

Text Edited: Marcia Lynx Qualey

Text & Cover Design: Nasser Al Badri

Cover art: Mark Songhurst / Alamy Stock Photo

JAN DOST

SAFE CORRIDOR

A NOVEL

TRANSLATED BY MARILYN BOOTH

Bait Al Ghassham DarArab International Translation Prize

Established in early 2023, this prestigious prize honors contemporary Arabic literature while fostering its global readership. It aims to showcase distinctive voices in Arabic literary authorship and translation, bridging cultural gaps and celebrating literary excellence. The prize is awarded in two categories:

1. *Translators' Category*

This category is dedicated to unpublished English translations of Arabic literary works originally written in Arabic and published in or after 1970. The winning work receives a financial award, which is shared between the translator and the copyright holder. The award also includes coverage for translation fees and ensures the publication of the translated work.

2. *Authors' Category*

This category celebrates unpublished Arabic prose and poetry, including novels, short stories, autobiographies, and poetry collections. Winners receive a financial award, and their works are published in their original Arabic and translated and published in English.

For more information, ccan QR code

To all of the children whose spirits have been mutilated by wars

These are the days in which I will die
My friends, may you meet your sacred task:
Hollow my grave at the foot of the rise
And plant me red roses along one edge
Seed some sweet basil down the opposite side
And then, friends of mine, guard my grave well
for my enemies are many
My friends, look here: the fear haunting me most
is the fear that my enemies will then appear ...
They will pluck all the flowers and strip the sweet basil
where you left it sleeping, upon my fresh grave

(from a folksong sung by the Afrin singer Jamil Horo)

Pale Chalk

On the evening when young Kamiran began to realise that he was turning into a lump of chalk, rain was bucketing down. The drops hitting the tent walls sounded exactly like the noise he remembered hearing in Afrin: volleys of bullets that rained down solidly for two days before the town fell to occupation.

Lying in bed, ready for sleep and just beginning to slide into its welcome sweetness, Kamiran sensed something odd going on. A change was coming over his body. He felt his feet going rigid: that was the first sign. Next, he had a peculiar sensation: that he was losing his toes, as if they were bits of chalk breaking off and dropping with a thud onto the mattress. Almost immediately, he felt something similar—and equally odd—happening to his legs. They were stiffening; and they seemed to have fused together.

Slowly—deliciously—the feel of it crept up over his body. Thighs to buttocks and then to his penis, as though it were just another little segment of hard chalk. His belly, his chest. He felt the fingers on both hands plop heavily onto the mattress, although they didn't make a sound. He could make sense of what was happening, he thought, only if he saw it as a horrifically frightening nightmare. And yet the boy felt no fear. He raised his head off the mattress—at least, he lifted it as much as his neck would allow, since at that very moment the stiffness had reached that far up his body.

Observing these changes to his own body engrossed him and chased his sleepiness away. He didn't feel particularly unhappy about what seemed to be happening. Indeed, somehow, this transformation gave him a feeling of enjoyment more blissful (as far as he could remember) than any he had ever known. Yes, he was aware that it was out of the ordinary to feel such intense pleasure at what appeared to be a conversion of his very flesh into hard calcified matter. But the strongest emotion he felt was a fervent hope that what he was going through right now would not come to an end—a longing that time would stop here, that he could hold onto these moments of gratification, grasp them with his fingers (even if his fingers had fallen off, like pieces of school chalk, to disappear into his bed).

In truth, matters had begun to take this strange course earlier, when they were still moving from place to place: he and his mother Layla, who never spoke now; his little brother Alan; and his Uncle Ali the bouzouki player. The four of them had left the town of Sharraan, which was not far from the Turkish border. They were fleeing the militias, wave after wave of detachments advancing on the heels of the Turkish Army. They took shelter with another brother of his mother's, Uncle Naasan, who lived in Afrin City and was quite a lot older. But then the divisions of the Turkish occupation forces reached Afrin and so they picked up and left again, in a great hurry. That was on the 17th of March 2018. At that time—and before that time, too—tens of thousands of civilians were on the run from the hellish Turkish bombardments. They were every bit as afraid of the militias who had allied themselves with Turkey, the ones playing their part in the wholesale strafing of the entire Afrin District. And so it ended, in blood and fire: the era of self-rule proclaimed by a Kurdish party in the north of Syria. The Turks saw that project of self-determination as an immediate and existential threat to their national security—and so could not allow it to continue.

The earliest signs of Kamiran's metamorphosis—which would take less than a month to complete—appeared when they were stopped near the military checkpoint outside the town of Kimar, on the way to the famous al-Ziyara Crossing. The tractor pulling them came to a dead stop. Kamiran and his family were packed into an open trailer along with several other evacuees, including a pregnant woman. Driving the tractor was Ali, whom everyone knew as Ali the Bouzouki Player, Kamiran's uncle. It wasn't the roadblock that stopped them. Ali stopped because that poor miserable woman went into labour suddenly, just before they reached the Crossing. It was clear that she was in a lot of pain.

On that same day, Uncle Ali discovered that the skin on his nephew's neck was so desiccated that deep cracks had appeared. He didn't know anything about the disease called calcinosis cutis. He didn't know that it targets the layers of skin just below the body's surface, nor did he know that various things can cause it, among them an excess of calcium in the blood. Neither did young Kamiran give this change any serious attention. It must be a simple ailment of sorts, such that he joked with his uncle about his scaly skin. 'I'm worried I'm turning into a fish.'

Day by day, the patches of afflicted skin widened and lengthened. His fingers grew as stiff and dry as firewood. The skin on his legs, neck, back, and buttocks, and even his penis, dried out. What was truly odd was that despite the skin condition, he didn't feel any pain. For that reason, the camp doctor, who worked for the Kurdish Red Crescent, didn't concern himself much with the case. He just handed Kamiran some painkillers whose only effect was to enflame the sarcasm of the concerned uncle and his sister's son.

By the time the dry-skin condition had more or less engulfed his body, Kamiran's yearning to write something had grown more pressing. But there was no proper place to write, and the surroundings were not hospitable. Instead, he began dictating his thoughts to his pale piece of chalk. He told her about everything that had happened during these years of war, across its harsh months, through its long days. He told her the secrets he had hid from his family. He gave vent to his feelings and to his fears: to everything that was apt to fill the mind of a boy on the verge of his teens living through the terrors of an insane war in a country where reason had lost its ability to steer the course of anything or anyone.

Now, as the later stage of Kamiran's transformation was drawing to a close on this rainy night, to the staccato sound of hard raindrops, his mother—forever silent—was asleep. He could hear her breathing, and it comforted him. His brother, who had been in agony all day from the intense pain in his hands and chest caused by the burns he had gotten that morning, was turning over restlessly on his mattress, muttering and grunting. And meanwhile, his Uncle Ali, the youthful bouzouki player, was sitting with his mates in a tent somewhere out there, some distance from their own, plucking his small lute and chatting the evening away as he usually did.

On this night, the boy was alone with his trial. He was on his own as the astonishing changes made their way across his body. Alone with this harsh pleasure that buffeted him like gusts of cold wind hitting his skin, from the tips of his toes to the parting on his scalp.

Kamiran wasn't thinking about what would happen in the next few moments—or about the fix he would be in when this small family discovered his condition. He didn't think about his mother, who would wake up the next morning and come to lift the blanket off him, ready to give his shoulder a shake as she always did, summoning him to breakfast. He did not think about his brother Alan who might come and sit next to his head, pleading with him to undo the dressings covering his burns and put on new ones, or letting him know that the burns weren't hurting quite so much now. He was not musing about his uncle, either—Uncle Ali, who might come into the tent at any moment, cursing the camp and Turkey and the war and the Party, as he had been doing ever since he came to live in this ill-omened place.

By now, he couldn't even see the ghostly shapes that had lived with him, a constant presence in his mind, since before this sequence of events had run their course and turned him into a giant length of chalk, 160 centimetres long. Inside of him, so very much had changed. Now he belonged to a different world, one where time didn't matter—or at least, time didn't seem to be like any of the other forces of nature. At the end of the day, here he was, an inanimate object, a huge piece of chalk inert beneath the heavy blanket, listening to the sound of the endless splats of rain that the storm relentlessly hurled against the matte-white outer skin of the tent.

Allow Me to Make Introductions

My name is *Kaamiiraan*. But you can just call me Kamran. In fact, you ought to say it like that, because it's more accurate. In Kurdish, it means 'the one who's blessed with luck'.

My mother used to be an Arabic teacher. Layla Aghazadeh. And my father—the surgeon, Dr Farhad. He was kidnapped by Daesh a few years ago, when we were still living in Manbij.

I don't think you know me very well, do you? No, even though you have lived with me for two years now, I haven't written very many sentences with you in my hand, not many at all, I'm afraid. Just a couple of shambolic slogans, I guess, like for instance, *Long live the Revolution.* Or a saying like *al-Jaysh al-hurr Allah yahmiih.* God protect the Free Army. That's what I used to recite over and over, along with my schoolmates at primary school in Manbij, before Daesh came to town. But I don't remember using you to write—for instance—*The people want the fall of the regime.* That was the sentence we kept on repeating back then, when we were walking alongside the adults in their demonstrations. Or there was the other one, *Your head will be eaten away* ... and you don't even need to say the rest: Your head will be eaten away, and that will make you as short and squat as my little brother's penis. He hasn't been circumcised yet, my little brother.

I stole you one day—it was sometime in the autumn. I was at school, and I stole you. I thought you were so elegant. Slim, shiny, and not like the other pieces of chalk, the cheap ones that came in white boxes with Directorate of Education of Aleppo stamped on them. Those 'government' chalks were fat and stubby, and whenever you tried to write with them, they made a cloud of dust. And the lines they made, when you wrote with them, were faint. You'd try to write out a word, and one letter would appear clearly enough, but then you could barely see any of the others. The chalk mutilated the word you were trying to write. One of our teachers—he was taken by Daesh later on—despised the chalk. He was so disgusted by that government chalk that he used to shout curses at it. One day, he was writing something on the board with a piece of that chalk when suddenly he threw it out the window. He said to us, coughing, 'A revolution has started, and things have changed in this country, but the chalk has stayed the same. *You* have to start a revolution now, one that's going to bring down this godawful chalk. Changing this chalk will certainly mean changing the regime, which can't for the life of it produce sound chalk that doesn't kill people off! *The people want the fall of the chalk---*'

'Now, repeat after me: *The people want the fall of the chalk.*'

We shouted this sentence until the chairs in the classroom were vibrating and all of us, all the pupils in the room, collapsed into laughter. The teacher slapped his hand against the table and ordered us to quiet down.

Laughter, yes—but it was a true disaster whenever the teacher ordered us to erase the chalkboard or when he wiped it clean himself. That white dust filled the whole classroom. We always had to throw the windows open wide and air out the room, even when it was the middle of winter. The white chalk dust settled stubbornly on the teacher's hair and got into his eyebrows and moustache. He didn't look like a teacher anymore; he looked more like the town miller. He was always trying to brush the dust off his work clothes and shake it from his hair. All the while, he would be muttering to us, 'I am going to die of asthma. This chalk causes asthma, it's worse than pollen or factory smoke. God's curses on the life of a teacher before the revolution started, and on his life after it started, too.'

Yeah, that's exactly what was going on, my dear, pretty chalk, my elegant chalk. *That's* what the teachers' chalk was like, the chalk that the government makes in its factories. But you, my own chalk, you came from somewhere else, somewhere outside the country! You were just lying there one day—that was the day I stole you. Yeah, just lying there, still and silent, and you grabbed my attention simply because you were lying there near the end of the green chalkboard. My hand shot out, I was just playing, really! And then I hid you, very quickly, but with a lot of care, I put you in my pocket and I took you home. But even now I still don't really understand why I did it. You were so appetizing, so tempting! Something, but I didn't know what it was, attracted me to you. Something pulled me there to the rim of the chalkboard. Maybe it's that I love to write, and I want to have *something* to say about everything that's going through my head.

But then, after I took you and put you in my pocket, you changed. You became just a plain little piece of something tossed into a corner of my room which overlooked the main street in Manbij. Just a little piece of something that no one would think twice about, except for me. I heard you complaining, every day I heard you. It was as if you truly were talking to me. Like, as if you were saying, 'Boy! Hey there! If you don't mean to write anything, then why did you bring me home like this? C'mon, pick me up and write something with me. Whatever you want to write. Just do it.'

So, things went along like that, until we were forced out of Manbij and we headed for Aleppo—about two years ago, I guess it was. We were on the point of leaving the house, I remember all of this really well, and suddenly something drew me to you—again. It seemed like there was some mysterious force at work, I had no idea what that was about. But I took you with me. Once we were there—in Aleppo, I mean—I forgot about you completely. I think I forgot you because I didn't find a single wall there on which I could write any of the sentences or phrases that were whirling about in my head. The walls in the neighbourhood where my grandpa lived, in Masakin Hanano, were either half-destroyed already or dangerous because they were on the point of collapsing. Or they were walls nobody could get close to, because you would see warnings posted on them, or posted somewhere nearby, left by some unidentified military authority. There was never any explanation to tell you why or how this wall was off-limits or where the orders came from. Anyway, most of the time I was too afraid of going out into the street. A lot of kids were dying out there. One of them was my beautiful little sister Maysoon. Children died of sniper fire, and bombs, and they died crushed beneath the ruins of their own collapsing houses. We saw it all, during the time we were living in Aleppo.

When it started, we really did believe that anyone who was dying in the war must be Army, or at least they were fighters of some sort. But then we discovered that the bombs and the missiles and the bullets—the damned fucking sprays of bullets that were louder than a megaphone when they got close—we discovered that they were one-hundred-percent blind.

Back when we were still living in Manbij, I always carried you around in my pocket. I was waiting for just the right opportunity to write out one of the things my father used to say. My father the surgeon, Dr Farhad. What he used to say before Daesh snatched him and he disappeared from sight and no one ever saw him again. There was one sentence my father repeated a million times in my hearing, and it really affected me. I knew it off by heart, as well as I knew the first verse of the Quran.

'All revolutions are alike, Kamran, my boy. They're just like ass droppings—you can't tell one from another. Or like hair—every one like its twin brother. Baara shaara!

I didn't understand what my father was getting at with this expression of his, but I learned it word-for-word anyway. And then my father disappeared. Just like that. We waited for him, we waited a long time. My mother waited for him. She began standing at the window every evening with Maysoon. They would peer out the window, eager to catch the very first glimpse of him, but it was never any use. Then my grandfather arranged to bring us surreptitiously to Aleppo. And from there, after my little sister Maysoon was killed in the bombing, we fled again, this time to Afrin. Running from one place to another I forgot about you, I kept forgetting about you. But even though you weren't inside my head and I didn't write anything with you, I never left you alone, not for a single day. No, I took you with me wherever I went. I guess there must be some secret to it, the way I take care of you. You're like a witch, my ghostly piece of chalk. I think *you* have some secret that you haven't told me, ever.

What I think is—I have to write my father's words of wisdom out somewhere. But where would I write all of it? Across my own palm or across the enormous behind of our neighbour Mazyat?

Of course, you wouldn't know our neighbour Mazyat, my dear chalk, my pale and slender friend. No, of course not. How would a piece of chalk with no features to speak of, and no feelings, get to know a village widow with such miserable luck and so much sex appeal?

This Mazyat was our neighbour back in Sharraan, the town near the Turkish border. I'm not going to tell you about her right now. It would just make your saliva run, and then I'm sure you would melt away. Yeah, you see, your saliva would come streaming out just as if you were a bitch in heat. Any talk of Mazyat and even the saliva of saints and pious men starts flowing.

Anyway, my girl, my slim little friend, this isn't the time or the place for talking about Mazyat's behind or the smell she gave off, which I'm sure would make heads swim even among the men on the other side of the border—the Turkish gendarmerie, I mean. I'll come back to it, this subject of Mazyat, when you and I are alone and when my brother Alan isn't with us, that little lice-shit who doesn't know how to keep a secret.

Maybe you are feeling really surprised that I'm talking to you only now instead of two years ago. Maybe you are saying to yourself, 'This boy is talking nonsense. He must have smoked a big wad of hashish or found some white powder to snort.'

Believe me, I haven't snorted anything except you. That smell of yours, which reminds me of the way the walls in our school smelled and of the sight of the chalkboard in our classroom in the primary school in Manbij, the town we fled from. I haven't inhaled anything except the pale dust you make, waves of tiny particles on which I can float. You are right, my dear, to object to my silence and my neglect of you for two whole years now. And then, well, why am I talking to you now when I didn't then? Because I was so stupid then that I believed a piece of chalk has no feelings and doesn't sense anything at all, and that she can't have any kind of relationship with a human being. I didn't know you, and that's why I didn't introduce myself or say anything to you.

It's the war, my friend. The war taught me that everything can feel. Even if it's the little bullet that bores into people's bones. It doesn't matter whether they're soldiers or they're ordinary people from town, still, that little bullet might be very sensitive—it might feel as much as the finger that presses down on the trigger feels as it frees the poor little bullet from its tiny cave in the muzzle. And just as the war taught me that everything has feelings, it taught me that a person's silliest, most trivial possession when they're in the midst of a war is exactly this—their senses, their feelings. In fact, it is even worse: it's their feelings that are responsible for whatever agony and horror they're going through.

Now I'm going to tell you a little secret. As secrets go, it's not really that important but I'm going to tell you anyway. Think of it as a confession from a kid who's scared of getting caught and punished. One day, I had the guts to poke a piece of cheap thick pasty-white chalk into the behind of the teacher's son. This was the teacher who showed up when the nice, funny teacher who cursed out the government chalk wasn't there anymore. I hated this teacher's son, I hated him a lot. He used to swagger around in the school courtyard because his father the new teacher was close to one of the Daesh emirs. One day when we were standing at the green chalkboard drawing tanks and helicopters, that boy said to me, 'Your dad was treating the men from the Free Army. Your father's one of the Sahawat.'

'Sahawat?' I echoed, but in a way that showed I had no idea what he was talking about. True, this was the first time I'd heard that strange word. Sahawat! But even if I hadn't heard it before, I understood immediately that this was definitely meant as an insult. At some point, I learned that it meant someone who didn't bow their head to Daesh, or maybe even who didn't help them. But even if I didn't know all of that at the time, I was still furious.

'My dad, Sahawat? Well your mama's a whore.' I had him by the collar now. The other boys stared at us, worried but also curious. They were in their seats, sitting 'properly'—that is, with their hands stuck under their armpits, the way we were all supposed to sit whenever the teacher entered the classroom.

The boy was wearing a blue track suit. I put out my hands and yanked the bottoms down, exposing his brown behind, soft and fleshy and darker in the middle. The bastard swung around to stand with his back to the chalkboard, trying to protect his backside from the curious eyes of his classmates who were darting looks at him, like arrows. But I jerked him forward to my chest and then, clutching him, I turned and forced him to stand with his butt facing the class so that all the students could see him exposed. They clapped and began shouting, and they were slapping their hands against their chairs. Then they split into two teams, one of them urging me on and the other supporting him.

'I'm going to fuck your whole family's daftar.'

I'd learned this insult from my Uncle Ali—after all, these daftars, these government-issued identity booklets that recorded marriages and children's names, were as precious as you could get. As I jeered at him, I was reaching for a piece of fat white government chalk, as thick and gross as the finger of a fat man. It was sitting on the bottom ledge of the board, exactly where you had been lying before, and then I had the wickedest idea.

'Give me one reason not to push this stupid second-rate chalk into his third-rate bum!' I said, addressing my classmates.

I didn't wait, though. The minute this thought came to me, I began trying to put it into action. But the scaredy-cat tightened the muscles around his asshole the way you do when you're trying to suppress an urgent need to shit. I began pressing my hands around his middle, squeezing as hard as I could until all of his muscles went slack. And suddenly I felt the chalk slide in. Half its length was between the cheeks of his rancid bum. I left it there and took a step back, waiting to see how he would react.

You're probably shocked to hear me talking so dirty, aren't you—my refined elegant chalky little friend! Well, that's who I am. *Kaamiiraan* who never shuts up, Kamran with the wicked tongue. I suffer from *verbal dysentery*—yeah, that's the doctors' word for it. I can talk without ever pausing, like a guy with terrible diarrhoea of the mouth. That's what my mother always used to say about me. That was before she was stricken with acute constipation of the mouth. I can talk for a whole week at a time about anything and about lots of things. Or I can go on endlessly talking complete nonsense. Sometimes this colossal gift for talking on and on surprises even me. Some of the women who came to visit my mother would get really fed up with me, now and then. I would be sitting right there among them, observing everything that was happening, and commenting on all of it, of course. Like, when they had finished their coffee and they turned their empty cups bottom-side up so that one of them could read everyone's fortunes in the coffee grounds. As soon as this woman started talking, I would start adding things to whatever she had to say. They did laugh, though, shaking their heads at the scale of my imagination and how good I was at making up stories, as smooth as if I were reading out lines written up there on the blackboard.

My mother always said that I was already talking in her womb. 'W'Allahi, Kamo, I could hear you! I was eight months into it. You'd be calling out *Mama!* there from inside my belly.'

Never mind, my lovely slender pale chalk. Don't think about my mother's claims or all her ravings. Let's go back to your chubby sister. Once I had poked her halfway into my enemy's butt, the rest of her looked like an unlit cig in the mouth of a puffy-cheeked chain smoker. That dog slunk out of the classroom, and I stayed up at the blackboard, fluffing up my feathers like a peacock, recharged by my resounding victory while all the other boys clapped madly. They were still cheering when I fled the next moment, never to return to that school. As I ran out dragging my heavy schoolbag, I could hear them whistling and clapping harder than ever, calling out my name with a pause between the syllables. *Kaa mi raan. Kaa mi raan. Kaa mi raan.*

I don't know what happened next. Did the chalk stay where I had pushed it in? Did it come out? If so, who pulled it out? Did what I'd done hurt him? How could he possibly go to school the next day? What did his father do? How did this man with all the Daesh connections treat his son and what did he do with this insult? Where did he get his revenge? Did he punish the students for supporting their classmate and cheering him on? If so, how did he punish them? Did he try to occupy our house like the Daesh people had been threatening to do nearly every day since my dad disappeared?

It was lucky for us that my grandfather arrived from Aleppo that same day. He took us—my mother, me, my little brother Alan, and Maysoon—to live with him for a few months. They were terrible months, really frightening, with constant shelling and a lot of destruction, and we always felt terrified. And then came the crying and crying for my little sister Maysoon, whose body was split in two on her birthday by a fragment from a barrel bomb. In those days, we were sobbing for my good sweet Gramma Nazli, too. She was hurt badly when the collapsing walls fell onto her, and then she was killed inside Jerusalem Hospital when the missiles exploded there and the hospital burnt to the ground.

Should I tell you about Aleppo, too? Maybe another time. Or maybe there's no need. After all, you were there with me in Aleppo—you were my companion, witnessing all the events we went through there until the moment we left for the town of Sharraan in Afrin District, and then you were with us when we left Sharraan to come to this crap camp where we are now.

The Letters of my Kidnapped Father

My dad's earliest letters appeared a month after he disappeared. The first one was only a few short, terse lines. I read them out to my mother.

Hello, Layla. How are you getting on? How are the children? Me: I am fine and carrying out my professional duties as usual. I don't lack anything except for seeing and spending time with all of you.

Don't try to ask about me. I will keep on writing to let you know I am well. I might be able to come home, perhaps sometime in the next two months. Take good care of the children, especially that little devil Maysoon.

I wrote that letter. It was in my handwriting. Reading it out to my mother, my voice was hoarse. My mother was an Arabic literature graduate, University of Aleppo. But I persuaded her to let me read these letters out loud to her so that I could watch her features and how the lines on her face shifted as I read each sentence.

So. I had copied this letter—with a few little edits—from an old book my father owned. It explained how to write letters. To give it a more convincing appearance, I inked it with the stamp my father always used on the prescriptions he wrote. I'd stolen it from his clinic next to the hospital. I figured this would be indisputable proof that my father really was the source. After writing that letter, I felt such relief and certainty, as though what was written in it really was the truth, as though it was reality and not just the wild imagination of a child.

As soon as I finished reading, my mother had a question ready. 'Who brought you this letter?'

I wasn't prepared for this question. It caught me off guard and I stumbled, I couldn't speak. Then I found some words. 'One of the Hisba men. One of the religious police.'

'And since when have the Hisba men become postmen for prisoners and their families, Kamo? Give me that letter, I need to see it.'

I handed her the letter, my hand shaking and my heart beating hard. I was terrified that she would find me out.

She turned the piece of paper over in her hands. She read the lines written there calmly and said, 'The handwriting doesn't look much like your papa's. If it weren't for the stamp, I wouldn't believe for a minute that he really wrote it. I'll match it up with his university notebooks. But why would your dad have taken that stamp with him?'

***

After my mother had examined the letter—and had been so surprised to see the stamp there, and had compared the handwriting (my handwriting) with my father's in his notes—she came back, kissed me on the head, and said, 'It's not so different. Probably your father wrote it in a big hurry.'

I was amazed to hear this. But all I said was: 'For sure, that's what he did. Not *probably*.' My mother just smiled. It was the first time I had seen my mama's beautiful smile since my father had been snatched and taken away.

***

That sweet smile that I hadn't gotten to see very often—and wasn't seeing at the time all this was happening—lured me into continuing the game. I got into the habit of writing a short letter—pretty much like the first one—every two weeks or so. It wouldn't contain any real information, and there weren't any expressions of feelings you might expect to hear from a husband. After all, I didn't know anything about that. So, it was always just a few lines, a hullo and a how are you and how are things going. And a little reassurance and a promise to be back soon. By the time I produced the fourth letter, my mother wasn't showing much interest anymore. She looked really sad and depressed. She hardly spoke to us. Also, she was imposing something like house arrest on us. She locked the doors and lowered all the curtains, even during the day, and she warned us constantly about hyenas and wolves prowling through the streets of Manbij and snatching adults and children alike.

We were totally irritated with being locked up like this by our mother the prison warden. All we could do—Alan and I—was to turn the house into some kind of gym plus playground. We bounced around on the sofa and did somersaults on our beds and more gymnastics on the Turkish carpet in the sitting room. We played hide-and-seek. We squawked and shouted and threw our sister Maysoon's dolls at each other. We used shoes and socks as footballs and we bent every rule we could. My mother was too deeply sunk into her griefs and her silence to care. There wasn't anything left for her in life, it seemed, except for her Maysoon, who would break out into sobs every so often, running over to the window or the locked door and wailing, 'Papa ... Papa.' When my sister got tired of that, she went back into the bedroom and played whatever it was she played.

As bad as we were, we did try to somehow lessen the pain we knew our mother was feeling. I would make animal sounds, trying hard to imitate them as well as I could, and I also mimicked the voices of the village women who used to come to my dad's clinic. Before, my mother had always laughed hard when I impersonated those women: how they spoke to my father and how they described their ailments. But she had forgotten what laughter was. Even with the funniest jokes, my mother stayed mute, her eyes gazing off in a direction I couldn't follow.

Then there was the day when we heard an insistent knocking on the door to our flat. Like we always did, Alan and I ran over to open it. But our mother had gotten there first, and she had made certain it was locked from inside. Only a few seconds passed before we heard the voice of my Uncle Nihad, my father's brother.

'Open the door—its Ammo Nihad here.'

We started shouting, that's how happy we were. 'Ahlan, Ammo Nihad! Mama's locked the door and she has the key.'

My mother came out of the kitchen, her face tight with worry. She didn't speak, but she waved her hands at us, I guess to ask who it was knocking at the door. 'Ammo Nihad,' we said.

To judge by her face, our mother's nerves were on edge. She reached for her satin kerchief, which was hanging on a wooden peg next to the door. She wrapped it around her head and stood at the door.

'Ahlan, Nihad. What's going on?'

'Umm Kamran, I have news of the Doctor—news I'm sure about. He's been locked up in the prison in Manbij but he's all right. Probably some interrogations or checks that have to be done, and after that he'll be able to come home and return to his work. That's all I've got.'

'Tayyib, Nihad. Fine, and God bless you.' My mother's voice sounded happy, but she wanted to go back to what she was doing in the kitchen. Alan and I trailed after her and began begging her to let us go off with Uncle Nihad to my gramma's house. My uncle could hear all the noise we were making, even from the other side of the door, and he began pleading with her, too. He promised he would bring us back in the evening. Finally, she agreed, but only on condition that he would return us here before sunset because—my mama said—that was when she would lock the door and she wouldn't open it for anyone, not even if it was Kamran's father himself.

***

On the way to my grandmother's house, Alan and I were celebrating the news about my father. We would run ahead on the street, dancing around, and then run back to where my uncle was walking behind us. 'My father's in Manbij now!' I said to myself, and then: 'I've got to change what the letters say, not the same old thing. He's in prison, he must be suffering, they must have tortured him. So, I should get him to talk about the torture and what the Daesh men have done to him—from the time he was taken until now.'

'No—there's something more important,' I answered myself. 'I've got to figure out a way to spring my dad from prison.'

The operation to free my father from gaol took over my brain immediately. I began walking silently alongside my uncle. I stared at the few cars that were coming and going down the long street, and I didn't say anything until we reached my grandmother's house. On the way back home, after staying away for about two hours, I was still thinking about my father's freedom and how to rescue him from the Daesh prison. I knew that the prisoners there didn't often come out alive.

***

Bismillahi ar-rahman ar-rahim

My Layla, I am writing to you from inside prison. I'm not far away. I think of you all constantly. Alhamdulillah I will be coming out of gaol because I've been cleared of the accusation that I was supporting the Free Army. They're going to let me out a week from now. My hugs and kisses to all of you.

Farhad

As always, I put the clinic stamp at the end of the letter and as I handed it to my mother I said, 'Someone—'

'Yes—someone from the Hisba brought the letter.' My mother finished the sentence I was intending to say. Then she kept speaking, her voice trembling. 'Son, Kamo my dear, do you really believe your mama is so stupid? I figured out on that first day that you were forging these sweet letters. I know you're trying to help, to make me feel better. I didn't say anything, and I didn't object because I've hoped with all my heart that a letter would come from your papa—letters like these ones you've been writing. I didn't say a word because I am very afraid for your father, and I was ready to believe any stupid little lie that might tell me he was still alive somewhere in this cursed world. But Kamran, my son, my heart is telling me other things. My heart doesn't tell lies, son. It never lies.'

My mother burst into tears. The three of us climbed onto her and clung there like little kittens, silent and still. Do you know, my pale friend, do you know the hurt that the families of the kidnapped and disappeared have to bear? Just ask me. It's a hurt like no other. Maybe it feels something like a knife that's been rammed into the heart and is waiting for someone to come along and pull it out. Or to treat the wound. Or to announce another death.

The Secret I Hide from Everyone

The sun came up.

What a lie. How can the sun come up when the sky is totally covered in dark clouds? What I meant to say is that morning came. Even better than either of these sentences would be to just say that I woke up.

So ... good morning, my pale chalk! First of all, before I do anything else today, let me give you a name. People name their dogs and their cats and their other pets—they give them very nice names, in fact. A long, long time ago, people used to name mountains and rivers and even the stars in the sky, coming up with all sorts of different names and descriptions. So why shouldn't I find a name for you that would spare me from always having to call you 'pale chalk'? Should I name you Sophie, for instance? Hunh? That name doesn't do it for you? Okay, how about Safra? It's a nice name, and the meaning comes close to your shape and colour. Fine, then, you are Safra. My little friend Safra.

Today, I'm going to tell you a few of my secrets. The first one is a really hateful, disgraceful one that I've kept from everybody for two years now. A secret that's not like any other secret, but I won't hide it from you, my pale chalk. Sorry, I mean, Safra. Because from this day on, you are the keeper of my secrets and my favourite friend. I'll tell you this secret right now, even though I am feeling super embarrassed about letting it get out. Didn't I say that it's a pretty vile secret, my friend Safra?

I wet my bed.

Yes, that's right, I pee in my bed. Every night.

You heard it. Every night, Safra.

But to this very moment, I haven't let anyone catch on that I'm suffering from *nocturnal incontinence*. Yeah, that's what they call this wicked thing, as far as I've been able to find out and from what I've heard. I haven't told anyone. Not my mother, and not anyone else, and not even you, of course, before now—and not our neighbour Mazyat, either, the one with the beautiful big behind. I used to visit her in her little house, but not even Mazyat got wind of my secret. No one knows what I'm going through.

Now, okay, I can imagine that maybe a question is flitting through your pale chalk-dusty mind. That question would be, more or less: How could something like that happen to this unlucky young fellow, Kamran? How could he hide his *incontinence* problem from absolutely everyone for all this time? In spite of all the moving around and living in different places? And where did it all go, anyway?—that urine his bladder was spilling out while he was fast asleep?

You've got a point there, friend. These are good questions—and there's another secret here that I haven't told anyone. But I'll tell you, because I know you are a mute, just like my mother, and you can't possibly tell anyone else, not even another piece of chalk, if you happened to meet her one day on a chalkboard or in the jacket pocket of a schoolteacher or even in the backside of a disgusting student like that bastard I told you about.

Well, what I do is, I put on a nappy before I go to bed.

Yeah, that's what I do, Safra.

A nappy to keep the pee from leaking out. But they're nappies I have to make myself.

Around here, there's not been a rag, or a bit of paper, or maybe a cotton undershirt, a piece of sponge or something similar, that I haven't picked up or stolen. Here's how it all happened. One day, I saw a green cotton robe hanging on an olive tree. It was giving off a sour smell you could pick up from a distance. Maybe it was some old person's stench, or housecat vomit, or something else, who knows? Maybe what I smelled was the shit of a fighter worn down by the war. Anyway, the cloth was dry and that was what mattered the most to me. I yanked it down from the tree and rolled it up and stuck it under my arm. That evening, I ripped a square piece out of it and stuck it between my thighs and wrapped it with a little bit of plastic to keep it from leaking. I went to sleep and my pee filled it. Yeah, when I'm asleep I don't have any sense of what's going on and I don't even feel it. When I woke up around 6 a.m., I took it off and tossed it away and no one knew a thing. That's been my routine for two years now, my dear Safra.

***

When this first started, I was sharing my little sister Maysoon's nappies. They were really small on me but they did the job. A little pee always seeped out but it wasn't enough to soak the mattress. Then my sister was killed by a fragment from an exploding barrel bomb that was dropped by a helicopter onto our street in Hayy Masakin Hanano before we fled Aleppo. After that, I had to find some other way to get nappies, and without my mother knowing about it.

There weren't many nappies around to buy that would be my size. Still, even the small ones were much better than any other stuff I could find. I started buying them from little shops. I always said I had a baby brother, so little he was still sucking milk from his mama. Until one day, when a shopkeeper from Aleppo said to me, 'Son, this size you're taking, it's for two-year-olds, even for children who are almost three. Your baby brother, how old is he really?' After that, and only by chance, I found a big store nearby where they sold 'nappies for older children'. When I read that ad posted up inside the shop, I was really surprised. These were nappies for children between the ages of five and eight. That's how I discovered I wasn't the only kid who was wetting their bed. Yeah, there were others who shared this terrible thing with me. This gave my head some relief.

So—I'm not the only one?

'In fact, the phenomenon of children suffering from *incontinence* has become impossible to ignore. Their number has increased greatly during the war.' I heard this statement one day from a doctor on a TV show who was talking about health and the war. He was being interviewed by a presenter with a huge bosom and heavy makeup, just like Mazyat's.

My friend, my Safra, do you know how such a thing happens? I mean, how a person can pee when he's asleep? You certainly haven't lived through anything like this. Can you imagine a chalk peeing in her bed? What a sick joke that would be! How can I be imagining these things, for the sake of the yellow devil! So annoying!

But you do pee. Yes, of course you do. Your pee is the writing you leave on the blackboard and on the walls of collapsed houses, and on the barrels that bring death, and on the empty shells that civilians set down in the empty space in front of their houses to use as flower planters, or to grow decorative green plants in them. It's their insane attempt to give the war the finger.

In addition to my father's famous saying—'Revolutions are as alike as one ass dropping is to another'—there's another saying that has been ringing in my head for the last four years. I want to write out this saying across every tank and cannon and military van. 'Fuck the War'. If it were possible for me to write those words everywhere, to write them even on the clouds and the sun that hides behind the clouds, on tree trunks and military boots and the helmets that soldiers wear, and before anywhere else on the barrels that the soldiers put up to make their checkpoints, and also on the barrels the airplanes sent hurtling down on us in Aleppo. Yeah. Fuck the War that has mounted down there, between my thighs, an out-of-order water tap where the water won't stop running. Fuck the War that sliced my sister Maysoon in half as if she was a biscuit, and stole my father and my house and my peace of mind and my school and my green bicycle. Fuck the War that—after we left Afrin—made it so that my home was a trailer pulled by a farm tractor that had to steer its way along a dirt track between the olive groves. Fuck the War that allowed hyenas and wolves to attack our last shelter in Afrin, stealing my sleep and my peaceful life, and the new habits I picked up in the town of Sharraan, when we were living with my uncles. Fuck this War that we don't know anything about. This war, that we don't know who lit the match that started it, or who will stop it, or when or how it will ever come to an end.

Now, I was about to explain to you, my pale friend, how it can be that I pee in my sleep almost every night. But I got distracted by Fucking the War, didn't I? This business isn't connected to the amount of liquid any one of us might drink before going to bed. No. If someone tells you that it is, then just say to them: 'That's a lie. It's pure malicious invention.'

It happens like this, nearly every night. First, I have a really nice dream. But very soon it turns into a nightmare. My bladder is full. I can feel it, it's like a bucket lifted out of a well that's spilling over with water, and it absolutely has to be emptied. I have to pee, I have a strong urge, and I look for somewhere—a public toilet, an empty spot, a tree trunk to hide me, a solitary wall, a lorry parked in a street where there are no people passing by, or any other place that could help me do what I really, really want to do—pee far away from anyone's eyes. Finally, I stumble on a remote patch of empty ground where no one will see me. It's dark and it's wet and there's the smell of urine already rising from it. I stand there gripping this leaky faucet that's between my thighs and I open it to its fullest, sharrarrarr shashasharrarr shashashashasha ...

A few seconds later, the nightmare is over. I feel a great sense of relief and comfort. I button up. Sometimes, I'm wearing trousers with a zipper that I have to do up. Anyway, the point is, whatever the situation, I turn around, feeling good about this place where I did my business, and then—

And then—I wake up.

Dammit.

I've done it again. In my bed.

'Never mind, boy', I tell myself. 'Just get that nappy off, quick, it's full of pee, and go toss it away as fast as you can, somewhere far away, before your mother wakes up.'

***

I'm telling you, Safra, my friend: This painful story of mine began on the day men from Daesh came to raid our house in Manbij, after my father was kidnapped. My father—the surgeon, Dr Farhad—gave an oath of allegiance, pledging to cooperate with Daesh out of concern for his personal life. And so that he could stay at his hospital and treat wounded and sick people. But then, one day, he disappeared, and we haven't found any traces of him since.

They didn't stop at kidnapping my father. They came to take the house, by force. Their beards terrified me and so did their baggy trousers, and I imagined their private parts dangling inside, like the wattle on a flapping turkey. I was afraid of their scary stares and their harsh language. When they spoke, there was no human sound to their voices. They threatened my mother, saying they would throw us out in two days' time if we hadn't left the house by then. They told her they would come and empty out the house and seize her by the arm and drag her out like a scabby bitch dog. That's exactly how they described my mother! They said they would take her whelps, too, and they meant us, they would take us as hostages until she obeyed the order they'd given her. My mother began to cry, and then to wail. We cried along with her. We'd crouched down in a corner of the living room and we were staring at them, scared, until they left—those God's soldiers and the men of the Islamic State, with their private parts, as I imagined, swinging left and right to a regular beat that echoed the rhythms of their fanatical anthems, war-songs meant to inspire their fighters.

It was that day. That was the day I was overwhelmed by a stupendous terror. An enormous fear, I can't begin to describe it, really. Or maybe more than a terror, what I lived through that day was a terrible, painful shock.

That night, I had a dream where a wolf was chasing me through a cruel landscape covered in snow as far as you could see. I was sinking into the snow and shivering from the cold and also shivering because I was frightened. This wild excited wolf was behind me, and the endless snow-covered land was in front of me. My knees were weak, soft, not strong enough to carry me. Suddenly I felt something warm running down between my thighs and all the way to the soles of my feet. When the wolf who was chasing me disappeared, I felt a huge sense of relief, I was calm again, and then I could hear my mother's voice calling me.

'Kamo! Get up, Kamo! Go and buy us some vegetables and meat.'

I woke up.

I was surprised to find my mattress so damp. I slid my left hand under the sheet to touch my pyjamas. They were wet. Then I realised that I had peed while I was sleeping.

'Okay, mama, okay', I said. 'I'm getting up now.'

She wouldn't leave me alone, though. She came over towards me, all the way to the end of my bed, and she raised the sheet off me. To this day, I still don't know how she discovered that I had peed in my bed. Maybe it was the sharp smell, or the dark patches the wetness made. The important thing is that she screamed as if she'd seen a snake. 'Animal! You aaanimaaal!'

She began spanking me, and slapping me, and cussing me out. Just imagine it, Safra! Imagine you open your eyes in the morning and what you have to face are slaps—hard slaps, one after another, and a stream of curses.

Aaah—awful, my friend, it was awful. I wish I were a chalk, like you. If that's what I was, it wouldn't even hurt me or bother me much to be stuck into the backside of the son of the Daesh guy, the teacher, all the way to the Judgment Day, just sitting there like a cigarette that hasn't been lit. That would definitely be better than this—peeing in my bed and then having to face being hit and insulted the minute I woke up. Completely surrounded by my sense of shame, so that I didn't know how to cover or hide.

I don't remember how I got myself up and out of bed that morning. Or what the look on my face said when I had to come up against my mother. My face must have been as heavy with the slaps I'd received as my pyjamas were heavy with piss. There was no limit that day to the humiliation I felt, I was so ashamed of myself. No end to the anger and resentment I felt at myself and at my mother.

The next day, it happened again. And the insults and slaps happened again. The shame I felt was right there again, the extreme embarrassment, the anger and resentment. All of it.

On the third day, it happened again, just like it had on the second day: I peed in the bed and there were more slaps and the rest of it. Luckily, though, my mother didn't tell my brother Alan what was happening to me. Alan was such a tattletale, that fasfoos! If she had told him about it, he would have told everyone. My mother always called my brother 'Monte Carlo' because of his incessant talk-talk-talk and the way he carried news from place to place and from one person to another. My brother Alan always tried to compete with me when it came to chattering away and letting all sorts of secrets out and telling tall tales. But no way could my brother Alan *defeat* me at these things. After all, I was the al-Arabiyya channel. I was al-Jazeera.

He was only a puny local broadcast station.

I started trying to think of some dodge that would rid me of my mother's slaps. At least. I didn't even consider the possibility of trying to stop the peeing from happening. I don't know why. Maybe because I sensed it was something I couldn't manage. But I tried to come up with another way to get rid of my mother's beatings. From those hands of hers that weren't showing me any mercy, from this mother who apparently didn't even try to ask herself why this peeing had started so suddenly, and without me wanting or meaning it, and over and over again, too, or to see that it wasn't my fault at all.

'I have to hide this disaster from my mother. I'm fed up with being slapped.' That's what I told myself. But for my mother not to start hitting me when I woke up in the morning meant I must not pee in my bed. Or, what it really meant was that I had to make certain no one had an inkling that it was happening.

***

My brother Alan was bewildered to see me exposed to these slaps every morning when it wasn't clear that I had done anything wrong. When he saw our mother hitting me, he curled up in his bed like a drowsy cat and didn't make a sound. Maysoon would burst into sobs, since she didn't understand what was going on either. Afterwards, she would creep over to me and try to comfort me, throwing herself into my lap and hugging me and trying to take my mind off it. I felt a lot of sympathy for her, and I would hug her back, and kiss her, and take her hand and lead her out to the street for a little while, and then we would come back inside once I could be pretty certain that the worst of my mother's nervous anger was gone.

My mother, who had begun to call me Abu Shakhkha, Mr Piss, didn't see anything to do about it except to spread a big piece of oilcloth under the bedcover to protect the wool-stuffed mattress from my pee. That was a good thing to do. It meant she didn't have to keep on dragging the mattress outside into the sunshine, or somehow exposing it to heat if we were in the winter, so that it would dry out. But my suffering got worse anyway. It's true that the treated cloth kept the urine from soaking the wool mattress. Instead, though, it all collected on top, making a shallow lake where I tossed and turned until waking up at dawn because the air was so cold that it chilled the pool of pee.

I was really, really ashamed of myself. It got to the point where I didn't even dare open my mouth to speak. I was no longer pushing my brother Alan around like I always had, and he sensed there was something troubling me. He noticed how distracted I was and how sad I seemed, and innocently, he began trying to comfort me. 'I know you're very sad about Papa. He'll come back, Kamo. W'Allahi l-'azim, I swear it, he'll come back. Come on, let's go out and play.' But I had lost my desire for playing or studying or anything at all. Every bit of my energy was going into my problem, and that blinded me to anything else that might be happening. It even made me forget about how anxious and scared I was about my father's fate in the hands of Daesh.

'There's no problem that doesn't have an answer.' That's what my father always drummed into me when he was helping me with my homework and could see I was hopeless at finding an answer to the problem I was working on.

So, then—there must be an answer or a solution to this abominable disaster of mine, too.

‘I’ve found it!!’ That’s what I almost shouted to myself one morning—a cold Friday morning, when I was getting some relief from the cold by standing under a lukewarm shower.

‘I’ll use Maysoon’s nappies.’ I said this in a voice I could hear clearly. I sounded like a guy coming up with some kind of ad copy for a famous brand of nappies. Before I went to sleep that night, I filched one of my sister’s nappies from the cabinet where my mother kept my little sister’s things.

After my mother had spread out the oilcloth that kept the pee from soaking into the mattress and had made the bed, she gave me a night-time kiss, and then she went over and kissed Alan. She left our room without telling us a bedtime story. This was her punishment to us for having been so naughty all day long. But I hadn’t cared much about my mother’s bedtime stories, not since I had had my own distressing story to occupy me. I got up and went over to my schoolbag and took out the nappy I had hidden there. I got back in bed. When I was sure that Alan had gone to sleep, I yanked off my pyjama bottoms and then my underpants and I did what my mother always did when she wrapped my little sister in her nappy. It all went so smoothly that I was amazed. True, the nappy was really tight, but I was able to make sure that the clinging rubber edge that went around my middle stretched across my skin well and closely enough that it would be impossible for the pee to seep out, no matter what. In my head, I was picturing the TV ads that showed children sleeping a happy sleep after their mothers had begun using a particular brand of nappy. Still, I felt so anxious. That was because I was so afraid someone would discover that I was stealing my little sister Maysoon’s nappies and using them myself.

I don’t know how I got to sleep that night. I woke up at dawn, as usual, after dreaming that I was peeing. This time, in my dream, I was doing it against the tyre of a big lorry standing in our street in Manbij. What startled me awake was the lorry's loud and irritating horn. But before I woke up, I could see myself in the dream, running away as I zipped my trousers up. Then I woke up and found that my hand was already shoved in between my thighs.

And then, what a surprise! There was only a slight wetness there. A thin thread of urine running down my right thigh. That was all. The nappy was completely saturated. It was very heavy and it felt irritating. I had to get rid of it, somewhere away from here, in the nearest rubbish dump I could find and as fast as possible.

It wasn't even light yet. It must have been about five a.m. Even grown men didn't dare go out into the street at this hour. But in this war, was it possible to talk about 'men' and 'children'? Was there such a thing as dawn or daytime? Never mind the worries about going outside—I would get this nappy off my body, I would wipe my damp thighs dry, and I would go out there, as bold as a true adventurer, to set this nappy full of pee down in the dark street, though not very far away from our door.

And so that's exactly what I did.

And then I came back into the room, very quietly. I was feeling high. Ecstatic. Like I was someone winning a war or making a revolution. Monte Carlo—my brother Alan—was still asleep, on his stomach, his face turned to the wall as usual. I lay down again, on my back, and counted sheep jumping over the river until I sank back into the river of sleep.

***

So, things went on like that, and my mother didn't seem to notice that there were fewer nappies in the cabinet. Things went on, that is, until a helicopter killed my little sister Maysoon on her birthday in Aleppo.

After that happened, my mother was completely absorbed by her grief. My grandfather and grandmother were completely gripped by worry for their daughter, my mother Layla, who had suddenly and wholly lost her voice after she saw her only daughter Maysoon sliced in two. But I was still absorbed in my odd and troublesome dilemma. I mean, this involuntary peeing at night. I used the rest of my murdered sister's nappies, and then, in secret and with whatever pocket money I had, I began buying nappies to cover my shame, which my mother no longer cared about.

Khadraa: My Green Bicycle

My father bought it in the bazaar—that's what Manbij people called the weekly Saturday souk, a very old tradition in our town. It was a green bicycle, a nice-looking one with a big headlamp on the handlebars and a small red light in back. Both lamps were powered by the little generator mounted on the hind wheel. The faster you went, the stronger the beam of light. The little bell on the right side of the handlebars needed only a light flick of my finger and it made a cheerful, friendly sound that alerted anyone passing by, especially anyone walking directly ahead of my bike, that they needed to move over and make room.

At first, my short bike rides were nothing more than rapid little circuits that took me from our house next to the hospital to Dawwar al-Sabaa Baharat to the west of us. It only took a few minutes. I came home without going by the main checkpoint maintained by Daesh at the Yunus Fuelling Station. Then my little excursions began to expand in time and space.

Khadraa—the Green Lady, as my father named that bike the day he bought it in the bazaar—became my companion. I treated her the way I treat you, Safra my friend. Anyway, this is the way I've been ever since I began to get wise to the world. I talk to these things around me, and I take them as my friends. I told my brother imaginary tales about them that used to astonish my mother.

'Kamo!', she said to me one day when she was completely fed up with my constant chatter. 'When you were born, you already had a story in your mouth that you just had to tell!'

Anyway, I loved that bicycle, which was my companion on all my outings, going here and there. On Khadraa, I went to the fields, and I went to the shops, and to the mosque and school and the bazaar, too. My brother Alan would run behind me, trying to catch up. I got a lot of joy out of seeing him collapse to the ground and burst into tears, because he couldn't go any further. Sometimes I let him ride behind me, but he was a scaredy-cat. He would put his arms around my middle and hold on to me so tightly that I couldn't steer the bike comfortably. He would press on my bladder so that I would have to stop after a few minutes. I would ask him to climb down and then I would get off to go and pee. After that, I would shoot off by myself as if I were a bird taking its first flight.

***

The day my grandfather came to Manbij to take my mother away from there after the Daesh people kidnapped my dad, I took my bike out of the building's cellar and wheeled it over to the taxi my grandfather had hired in Aleppo and brought to Manbij.

'Son, what are you doing with this bicycle?'

'I'm taking it to Aleppo with me, Grandpa.'

When he heard these words from me, my grandfather's face darkened. His eyes began shifting between my bicycle and the boot of the taxi. He was about to say something when the taxi driver spoke up.

'It's a small bike, Uncle. The boot's big enough. Don't worry, we'll take it with us.'

It made me really happy to see the driver take the bike from me and lay it down in the boot. I felt as if in some way I had rescued a precious spirit from nearly drowning in a deep river. I even got the feeling that I was somehow freeing my father from his kidnappers.

'My bicycle's going with me to Aleppo! It'll take me through all of Aleppo's beautiful streets.' I said this to aggravate my brother Alan, and I felt no end of delight in saying it, without either of us knowing what the sniper called Fate was sketching out for us there.

***

'Beware! Sniper!'

In Aleppo, I saw a lot of streets decorated with this shit sentence.

'Grandpa, I want to ride my bike.'

'No, son. The whole world out there is war. Missile strikes and snipers shooting people.'

'Missile strikes and snipers? What's that got to do with me? Does the war outlaw riding your bike?'

'Wars outlaw life itself, son. War keeps you from steering your own legs and feet, so then—steering your bike? You're still a child. When you're older, you'll understand what war really is.'

My grandfather didn't realise that we children are the people who best understand what war means. It's we children who know wars as they really are, not the adults. Probably my grandfather, and many other men, were thinking about their businesses more than they thought about anything else. Their minds were on shops, olive groves, olive oil presses, or some other interests they had. Maybe he was thinking that a little bicycle had no value or meaning to anyone in a great big war that was destroying everything, like this war of ours in Syria.

But to me, this little bicycle was more valuable than a village that the So-and-sos had just liberated—and next thing you know, the same village was liberated by some other So-and-sos. What I cared about was this bicycle and the hours of good fun I spent on it. I didn't care about who was ruling or who was in opposition or who controlled that checkpoint or who led this militia or that division. All I wanted was for us kids to be left in peace, to play and go to school and work on our hobbies in complete freedom and far away from the grownups' stupidities and their shit-eating ways.

You grownups! You didn't breed us in order to shove us into your dirty adventures. Or to dump on us your despicable hatreds, which seem to have no end. We get it: we know pretty well that bringing us into the world was nothing more than the natural outcome of your appetites and lusts. So, I guess you don't wish any of this on us, but then, you just assume that we're just kids who don't know anything at all. But we aren't like your generation, standing in endless queues to get a packet of bread or a box of tissues or a tin of baby formula or a gas cylinder. What I mean is, we don't have to agonize over a lot of the stuff that you did. We're the generation of the mobile phone and the internet and things you don't even know about. We know very well what war means, and what it means that we're fleeing from place to place like a cat who has to carry her kittens in her mouth as she scurries from one spot to another.

My kitten was my little bike that kept me company from Manbij to Aleppo, where I couldn't ride it because of the missile strikes and the snipers.

When we fled to Afrin District from Aleppo and then settled in the little town of Sharraan, which seemed peaceful and secure, I began riding through the streets and going around the squares, and even out into the fields, with nothing to stop me. One time I got as far as the village of Sinka, and then my musician uncle Ali began taking me to the village of Jaman and Ali Bazanli, on Maydanki Lake. We would come back to Sharraan after a very pleasant two hours out.

One time, I started out on my bicycle, following a big procession that was making its way toward the village of Metina. Curiosity pushed me—along with some of my friends—to join this procession on our bikes. Colourful flags were snapping in the breeze and the fighters in their camouflage were raising their fingers in victory signs and shouting. 'The martyr doesn't die! The martyr is not dead!. There were women crowded into jeeps and the backs of pickups, some crying, others trilling, and still others clapping and singing. It was a spectacular sight to see, astonishing in fact, and well worth following. When that curious procession reached the village, it swerved off in the direction of a huge graveyard. The cars and jeeps and trucks came to a stop, converging on still other vehicles and another whole crowd of people who were already here at the gravesite. I found out that it was a memorial procession for some fighters. We propped our bikes against the cemetery wall near the gate and went to join the masses of people who had flocked there.

The corpses of five martyred fighters were laid out on the ground, in front of graves that had already been prepared. The biers were draped in the flag of the Kurdish People's Defence Units, the Yekîneyên Parastina Gel, and there was a colour photo of each martyr fixed onto the front of his coffin. I saw women wearing black throw themselves onto the coffins and sob, while a man with a very thick, heavy moustache spoke, threatening revenge for the blood of the martyrs.

I was standing near two old men who were talking to each other in whispers. I found myself straining my ears to hear them so that at least I could get the gist of what they were saying. One of them, blowing his cigarette smoke into the air, said, 'They're sending them to their deaths, wholesale, all together. And then they bury them one by one.'

'So, what are they supposed to do?' asked the other elderly fellow, who was also smoking furiously. 'Every nation pays the cost of defending its borders.'

The first man responded, and you couldn't miss the ridicule in his voice. 'Are there any nations left anymore? Say instead: there are graves and shrouds.' Then he went silent as the fighters committed the martyrs to the soil, calling out all the while, 'Martyrs do not die! Martyrs are not dead ...'

I moved away, leaving the two men inside their tent of cigarette smoke. A fighter who must have been about twenty years old came up and patted me on the head a bit roughly. 'Hey there, comrade! What about you—don't you want to become a fighter and get revenge for the blood of the martyrs?'

I didn't answer. It scared me, the thought of carrying a gun and going off to fight. I love going around on my bicycle, riding through the fields. I don't want to meet death on the killing field. I'm a little kid who still pees in his bed. I'm not fit for the grownups' wars. I've heard that a lot of children have gone to the battlefield and that they never come back.

But let's leave aside all this painful kind of talk, my chalk-friend. Let me go back to my own trivial little business. Trivial in the grownups' eyes, of course. I mean, my little green bicycle.

***

In the first days of March, one wave after another of Turkish Army troops advanced on the town of Sharraan. My mother was very frightened. She would hug us close and start sobbing. I couldn't stand it when she cried like that.

'Nothing will happen', I would say to her. 'Trust the comrades.'

There were fighters here who would defend us. We wouldn't become dinner for the wolves. She stuck out her tongue to show what she thought of my words. I realised she didn't feel trusting at all, when it came to the guys who were defending us. On Tuesday, before the end of the first week of March, the units of the Free Army who were funded by the Turkish Army reached the Sharraan police station, and within hours, they occupied it.

That hadn't been what people expected. People were always talking about tunnels and barricades and fortifications that would keep even the biggest armies from successfully attacking the town. I remembered the words of that man standing near the coffins of the five martyrs. He'd said that they had weapons and provisions enough to last them ten years.

We had no choice but to flee again.

'The bicycle!' Those were the words I cried out to my mother, a lump in my throat nearly choking off my voice. She waved her hand at me, telling me to start walking, and then she put the index finger of her right hand to her dry lips, and I understood that she wanted me to be quiet. It was very early morning. She was holding my brother Alan by the hand and leading us away quickly, without a single glance behind her.

Did it make any sense that I would leave my bike behind and flee without it? Did it make any sense for me to betray Khadraa and turn my back on her? Why couldn't I bring her along with me? I would have steered the bike carefully, and I would have ridden very slowly, and then I could have avoided the pains in my feet that were already beginning to keep me from walking any faster. For a whole hour, the questions tore at me like the warplanes were tearing at the skies over Afrin. After that, we arrived at a spot near a village my uncle said was called Mashaala. Then we turned west on the Afrin Road. My Uncle Ali had done what *he* wanted, grabbing his instrument before we left and bringing it with him. Whenever we took a short rest, he would play cheerful songs to help us forget what hard work it was to migrate like this. But then, why hadn't I been able to bring my bicycle?

'Forget about Khadraa, Kamo. This is like the Last Day. The Day of Judgment.' That's what my Uncle Ali said during one of our brief stops as he was tightening the strings on his pretty bouzouki.

'That's got nothing to do with me', I said, my voice resentful. 'If Khadraa were with me, then I wouldn't care if it was the Last Day or not.'

Uncle Ali smiled. 'Don't grieve over her. I promise you, I'll buy you a new bike when we get there.'

'Get where?' I was still feeling very annoyed, and my voice showed it.

'To Afrin, you, Your Uncle's Little Puppy. To Afrin.'

'So, then what happens after that—Your Puppy's Uncle?'

'What do you mean?'

'I mean, if those militia units and their Turkish Army backers get to the city of Afrin, where do we go then, Uncle?'

'To flaming Hell!' My uncle's voice was angry. He finished adjusting the strings and sang a sad song by the Kurdish singer Jamil Horo.

***

From there, we walked for more than two hours. I got very tired. My mother was exhausted. She and Uncle Ali took turns carrying Alan part of the time so that we could get there more quickly. We were afraid of being targeted by the Turkish airplanes that were hovering up there in the sky, as if what they were really chasing were the long caravans of refugees. When Uncle Ali was carrying Alan, I had to carry the bouzouki on my shoulder instead of him, and I walked with a little swagger in my step, strutting as if I were a musician who was very pleased with his instrument. Meanwhile, my mother was bent under the weight of her big embroidered bag, and I could hear her moaning.

We weren't alone out there. There were thousands of people who were fleeing like we were. They were coming from other villages, carrying nothing except their children on their backs and small bags slung over their shoulders or sitting on top of their heads. No one knew what was actually in all of those bundles and bags. Everyone was cursing this state of things that we'd all come to, and cursing the people who had gotten us into this condition.

'Damn them, whoever it is that's the reason we've had to find our way through these wild empty lands where we don't know where we're going.'

Those were the words people repeated most often on that day. But I just kept repeating the sentence that suited me best. 'Fuck the War.' Until my uncle, teasing me, said, 'WAllahi, nephew, it's the war that has fucked us.'

***

After a long and exhausting journey, after hours and hours of walking, we arrived in Afrin on the fifth of March.

'It's chaos!' That's what my uncle spat out when we got there and saw how crazy the situation was. The place was heaving with people, migrants from all over—villages, towns, and hamlets. People had fled from everywhere, heading for Afrin City as a refuge. As if Afrin was the citadel that would protect them from the evil of these raiders.

On my mute mother's face, I could see a look that seemed to suggest happiness. The joy of arriving in the land of security. Reaching a safe shore. Getting another lease on life, maybe. For being somewhere you could feel a little hope.

'We're staying with some relatives.' That's what my uncle said. I'd never heard that we had relatives anywhere in Afrin. They were my mother's maternal uncles.

On that first night in Afrin, I couldn't sleep. I was so embarrassed and anxious, knowing I might pee in my bed, that I stayed awake until very far into the night. Then I got up and went out to pee. An hour or two later, I woke up from a light and fitful sleep to go and pee again, and so it went until morning.

The Widow Mazyat

When we moved from Aleppo to Sharraan in the autumn of 2015, we had moved in with my Uncle Ali the musician, who had in his turn moved into the home of one of his maternal uncles. That is, the home of one of my Gramma Nazli's brothers who had emigrated to Europe years before.

It was a beautiful house with a lot of space. It sat near an olive grove that went on and on. We were ecstatic about coming out of the prison of our cramped flat in Aleppo. Our Uncle Ali really paid attention to us and our needs. He also got hugely irritated at the naughty things we did and all the commotion we made. He tried to silence us by playing plaintive songs on the bouzouki.

My mother was as silent as ever. That is, ever since Maysoon's murder, she hadn't uttered so much as a single letter of the alphabet. She was 'a basalt boulder.' That's the way my Uncle Ali always described her, sounding sad. He kept on playing the sweetest melodies he could think of for her, the ones she loved, the ones she always asked for back when she was a university student. Like the songs of Fairuz, and Lina Chamamyan, and Mayada Basilis, and some of the Kurdish songs that were my father's favourites. But the only way my mother responded to his bouzouki playing was with tears running down her very pale face, and a sad weak little smile.

Every try ended in failure. Even a neighbour woman's attempt to take my mother to see a well-known shaykh for a cure—that failed, too.

Our neighbour's name was Mazyat. She was a twenty-five-year-old widow. She didn't have any children from her short marriage. That's what she told me.

Her husband had been a soldier in the Syrian Arab Army, the government's military. He was killed at the start of the war in a battlefront in Homs. She inherited the house from him. As a widow, she had a fierce reaction to anyone carrying weapons and shooting bullets. She tried (as she told me) to kill herself, but she didn't get it right. Then she tried to escape, like a lot of other people did. She tried to cross the border and get to Europe, but she couldn't manage that, either.

One winter morning when Mazyat came over to the house we were living in to visit my mother, what grabbed my attention was her perfume. It was bewitching, that piercing smell. I'd never smelled a perfume so pure and strong. True, I couldn't tell one brand of perfume from another, but I understood somehow that this particular scent was supposed to do something more than simply give a woman an arresting smell. It was a perfume that got things done. When it hit me in the nose it made me go hard, like a fat chalk. I pressed my thighs together hurriedly to hide my hard penis from Sayyida Mazyat, the good woman who had come to help my mother in her heavy ordeal.

***

It was good luck that the shaykh who our neighbour Mazyat promised my mother would cure her of her inability to speak fled from Sharraan, once people found him out. The party comrades threatened him with death if he went back to conning poor women. He disappeared almost immediately. And ever since, our neighbour

Mazyat had been a friend of the family. She started coming around every day to visit my mother. Mazyat would always try to comfort her and to show how much she cared.

My silent mother also visited Mazyat, going there to drink tea and eat the delicious Kurdaghi foods that the pretty widow made for her. Foods of 'Mountain of the Kurds', which was what we called the Afrin region. There were many occasions when my mother took me—me and Alan—along to Mazyat's house. We would play in the courtyard and climb the cypress tree and throw a ball back and forth until it was time to go back to our house. The days passed in this way, and then it was the new year. I mean, the beginning of 2017.

New Year's Day morning turned out not to be an ordinary day. Snow had been falling since dawn and it filled the whole world with a sharp and splendid whiteness. That morning, we visited our neighbour Mazyat after she texted my mother, telling her to come and visit, and they would drink coffee together. Alan and I had fun walking over the snow and listening to the pleasant, rhythmic crunch our feet made as they sunk partway in. We began jumping around in the cold air, trying to grab the snowflakes that were flying and drifting along like white butterflies or daisy petals that floated over the fields.

Mazyat's house was warm. That wasn't exactly common around here. I'd often heard my musician uncle say, when he was complaining about how scarce diesel fuel was, that most of the time there wasn't any oil available at all. Then he would cuss out the Free Army.

'Fuck the Diesel-Oil Army. Fuck the freedom that will come by cutting off oil supplies to civilians.'

The battalions of the Free Army based in Izaz and other areas, which were cut off by the siege on Afrin, were from time to time very intent on trying to cut off the routes for the fuel supply chain. This forced people to resort to smuggling fuel and selling it for unbelievable, astronomical prices. My uncle didn't forget to curse the Party. According to him, it was also a partner in all of this—these forces that were drawing the map of suffering for civilians and exploiting the war for aims that weren't innocent in the slightest.

Mazyat gave us a warm welcome, hugging and kissing my mother and then hugging my brother Alan. When my turn came, she held me very tightly and pressed me to her chest. I could feel the softness of her round breasts. The scent of her perfume burst from her neck and chest, and it just about plunged me into a state of total bewitchment. She went on hugging and kissing me for so long that I began feeling like she wanted to bring me inside this soft body of hers. I went hard. I was so embarrassed! 'Down, silly,' she whispered to my thing, but it didn't want to flop down. Mazyat was still holding me and my wicked member kept getting longer. I felt this strange pressure. It felt really good, so good I can't describe it.

Mazyat let go of me after pouring an *aaahh* into my ear. That was not something I was used to hearing. It made me feel dizzy; it felt really good. I sat down next to my mother, my feelings all confused and impossible to understand. What had this woman who was more than ten years older than me done with me? What was happening to make my stupid penis into a fat hard chalk that didn't want to go limp? I lowered my head and stole a look at my trousers. In the space between my thighs, there was a little wet stain. I was afraid it was pee. But I didn't pee in my pants during the day. So, what was this about?

I stayed in this dreamy state of distraction, like I was sinking into the depths of a nice, warm, dark river. I seemed to have gone mute just like my mother, who looked happy at being with her friend.

Alan, though, went over to the window to stare out at the snow that was still falling. Then he came back and stuck his hands out above the woodstove to warm them up. After that, he wandered from one corner of the house to another. Several times, when I raised my head, my stare collided with Mazyat's. There was a strong glint in her eyes. They looked like rays of sunlight that burned into me. I started getting hard again, and I was feeling that odd sense of pleasure. In order to avoid that shot of desire in Mazyat's eyes, I had to lower my head again. I stared hard at the patterns in the beautiful carpet we were sitting on, our backs propped against pretty feather pillows.

More than an hour passed. This very nice widow gave us tea and sweet biscuits and savoury snacks and we stayed until my mother began to yawn. The sitting room was so warm that it made her sleepy. She gave Mazyat one of her own special signs, putting her left hand over her right hand, dropping her head and cradling it in her hands to show that she wanted to go home and sleep.

Ever since we had come from Manbij to Aleppo, and then after my grandfather took her to the doctor, my mother had taken sedatives that made her fall asleep. I had been diligent about handing those pills to my mother. I thought they were just medicine to treat the awful muteness, until my uncle told me that they were meant to calm her nerves and help her to get to sleep at night.

***

Mazyat insisted that we stay on with her. She brought out a big, heavy Turkish blanket and draped it over my mother, telling her to go to sleep there next to the woodstove. My mother didn't object. She even beckoned Alan over to take a nap in her arms. It was only a few minutes before the two of them were fast asleep. Mazyat winked at me and smiled.

'Don't you want to sleep, too, Kamiran?'

'I don't take naps during the day.'

'Would you like to play something on the iPad?'

'iPad? What's that?'

'Don't you know what an iPad is? It's something like a mobile, only bigger. Come on, you can see it. There are some really nice games on it.'

She got up and walked into another room. I could watch her big behind, quivering. I followed her like that mythical guy afraid of the hyena, who follows it into its den instead of running away. We were in her bedroom. I knew that because there was a big bed in there covered in pretty sheets. Going over to the window and pulling down the shades, Mazyat said, 'Sit down and I'll bring you the iPad.'

I looked around. I couldn't see any chair in the room. So, I had to sit on the edge of the big bed. She was busy searching the drawers at the bottom of the elegant wardrobe, looking for this iPad which I was now keen to see. Her body bent over, her buttocks shook like two big globs of gelatine. She straightened up and came toward me, but there was nothing in her hands.

She sat down next to me on the bed. Her voice sounded apologetic. 'I'll find it, for sure. I'll find it. Just this morning I had it in my hands. I guess I've forgotten where I set it down.'

Suddenly she pulled me to her chest and began kissing me on the mouth. My heart was pounding so hard I thought it would come careening right out of my body. As she was kissing me, Mazyat was pulling off my woollen jumper. Then, with a sort of acrobatic little movement, she planted her hand on my trouser zipper and unzipped it and lifted out my penis.

I didn't know what to do. I was completely stunned by what was happening. She gripped my right hand and lifted it to her chest, then she put it on each of her breasts, first one then the other, and began moving my fingers over the nipples. I could feel them harden like a pair of new rosebuds. And then I didn't have any idea about anything, until I found myself lying down next to her, and I was completely naked. She was breathing hard and saying some naughty words. She pulled my hand away from her chest and brought it down to where her thighs met, and then she raised it again to her chest. Her hands began tugging at my backside so hard that it hurt. But all of this went along with a mind-blowing feeling of pleasure that ran through my cock and made it as hard as the barrel of a cannon about to fire.

I didn't know how I was supposed to behave. My feelings were in a total jumble—shame, embarrassment, thrills, fear, astonishment. But only a minute or so passed before Mazyat had turned over and was lying on her back. She pulled me on top of her and took hold of my cannon barrel and stuck it between her thighs. I went inside Mazyat. Everything was wet. She began gripping my buttocks and pulling me towards her, and then pushing me away from her, lightly, pulling me and then pushing me, again and again, as she moaned, making a sound sort of like a quiet sobbing. Then she left me alone and I found myself making the same movements on my own, in a regular and quickening rhythm until there were odd sounds coming out of both of us.

The storm let up. I was lying on her chest. I was afraid and I was happy. She was biting at my ear, light little nips. She kissed me and wrapped her arms around me.

'Hey little fellow, you really wanted it. Like a real man.'

I didn't have anything to say to that.

'Don't feel embarrassed, little guy. Today, I've made it official: you're a man. We can keep on living inside these honey-sweet moments if you want to. You just have to keep it a total secret. My secret and yours. No one has to know about it. Okay?'

'Okay.' I was calm, pulling on my clothes. She got dressed, too. I was too embarrassed to actually look at her body. She grabbed my head and made me turn it to look at her. She kissed me on the neck.

'Did you like the iPad?' she asked, giving me a wink.

***

Like a thief, I came out of the young widow's bedroom on tiptoe. I saw my mother and my brother still fast asleep, covered in the Turkish blanket, in exactly the same position we had left them in about an hour before. I sat down near my mother's head and began staring into the woodstove's flame, which was capering around like a shameless dancer.

Mazyat had stayed in her bedroom, humming a tune by Bahija. I could hear the sound of curtains being pulled by that delicious woman, and then I heard the screech of the windows opening to air the room and let its rude fumes escape.

I was still deep inside my thrilling excitement, the moments of extreme pleasure I had just lived through on that bed. It's a thing that doesn't really allow description, my chalk friend. If that chubby white chalk that I stuck into the bum of the teacher's son one day were here, no doubt it could describe for you the pleasure of going inside, and thrusting yourself even deeper.

***

I had a lot of days like that one. I got addicted to visiting the gorgeous sexy widow Mazyat. She cursed the war in a kind of hysterical way. One time, she asked me, 'Do you know what war means, my little sparrow?'

'No, I don't.'

'War means that this lock has no key.' As she said these words, she put her hand down to the crack where her thighs came together. Then she reached for my penis and, laughing, she went on. 'Your key's a nice one, handsome and firm, my little bird, but it's small. I'll make it grow until it fits inside my keyhole perfectly.'

***

For months, my life in Sharraan was tossed here and there by the surging river of honey that ran through the bedroom of the widow Mazyat, my eager desirable lover. Yes, my pale chalk; yes, Safra my friend, when I say 'eager' and 'desirable', I know exactly what I'm saying. Mazyat was a very pretty woman. The griefs of her widowhood added a layer of beauty to what was already there. You didn't see her breasts—so round, and dripping honey and sweet cream. You didn't see her buttocks—trembling like two winking stars shining huge in the vastness of the dark sky. You didn't see her bright-red lips, and you never heard those aching *aaahhs*. You didn't touch her chest—soft and smooth, as though it were polished; you didn't push your fingers into the damp forest between her firm thighs. But I ... lived all of it. That widow opened my eyes to the arts of body-war when I hadn't known a thing about any of it.

That's what Mazyat called our times together. She would say: 'In our body-battles, my little darling, it isn't about 'this one wins and that one's defeated'. Listen carefully. It's true, there are two parties. There's the war, and there's the body. But the one who wins out over war is always the body. You and me together, Kamiran, and our bodies, which will disintegrate and disappear, we're the ones who win in the battle of bed vs. war—Umm al-Sharmuta! This whore-mother's war. The front we're fighting on is this king-size bed, my little starling, ya zurzuuri, and the two warring sides are our bodies, yours and mine, and we win the war whatever happens. There's no revolution except the one that flares up on the bed. Any of the other revolutions are just fakes. The two of us are the victims of the rich people's quarrels that they pick amongst themselves. The bed is the battlefield where we get our revenge on them—on the executioners. Got it?'

The arts of combat on the bed front weren't the only thing that Mazyat taught me. She also taught me how to smoke. And she taught me other things I'd been totally clueless about before that snowy day when we came together. At her home one night, I drank a kind of araq called al-Batta. That was a night to remember. For the first time in my life, I got drunk. It was the evening of the Eid al-Fitr. Summer weather. Mazyat had invited my mother to come over for the holiday celebration, and she begged her to stay through the evening and spend the night. I went along with my mother. She and Alan went to sleep in the sitting room before ten pm. Then the beautiful wolf dragged me into her den and poured the alcohol for me.

After a second glass, I couldn't see straight. I don't know how that night ended. What I do still remember—clearly—is that Mazyat nearly swallowed my dick. Or she nearly bit it off, I think. When I woke up the next morning, I remember, I had a terrible headache. And I was stunned to find that I hadn't peed in the bed.

Ambushes for Blind Feet

On Tuesday morning—it was the 20th of February—enormous crowds gathered in Azadi Square in Afrin. It used to be called Old Palace Square, according to my Uncle Ali. There was a journalist with a good-looks face and a good-family name who had come here from the capital to raise people's spirits. People clung to him like drowning bodies clutching at the rim of a rowboat. In him, they saw a saviour who would rescue them from the Turkish flood, a shield to defend them against the blows of the Turkish Zeytin Dalı campaign. They fell on him, all of them wanting to take selfies to commemorate the moment.

'Instead of sending us tanks and planes, they've been so generous to give us this idiot? If this journalist can save his own behind, then it's our duty to hand him a medal for being so brave. First class honours!' That's what one old man called out, but his voice was lost in the vast surging sea of the crowd's roars. People were still pouring into the square and shouting slogans. The masses of bodies in that space lifted the smiling journalist onto their shoulders and kept up their shouting.

'Total insanity!' my uncle shouted. 'Collective hysteria, that's what it is.'

The loud voices got even louder. On the television screen, we followed their noisy celebration of the journalist's arrival. They looked like they were responding to my uncle's shouted words, and he screamed into their angry faces with a voice that was even stronger and louder.

'The traps have been set with perfect planning, and your feet are blind.'

None of the people who were pressed in there answered him. The slogans welcoming the handsome journalist shot into the air, and the flags and photos in people's hands did a jig.

'Wajh in-nahs', muttered my uncle. 'That guy is bad luck.' Uncle Ali was getting more and more irritated. He was so angry by now that he almost turned his expensive bouzouki into a club and slammed it against the ground. 'Asses. Asses, and the stakes they've been tied up to have been ripped clear out of the ground.'

***

But no one paid any attention to my uncle as he went on swearing at the crowds massed in Azadi Square. After all, these days, people would go on celebrating for hours over the arrival in Afrin of a unit of reserves from the Syrian People's Army.

Suddenly, my uncle laughed in a manner I wasn't used to hearing from him. Not laughter so much as it was a series of hysterical squawks. When he got quiet, he wiped away the two big tears that had spurted from his eyes. Then he raised his head from his mobile phone so that he could show me a sentence published by one of the Kurdish writers on his Facebook page. Just a line, welcoming the Syrian Amy. It shook the whole being of my musician uncle as if it were an earthquake.

'Greetings to the Syrian Arab Army, which is protecting the Kurdish olive groves from the filth of the attackers and the impurities of their servants.'

'This bastard writes like a whore who might be a whore, but she likes one dick better than another. He's an f-ing prostitute sharmut who hasn't had enough fucking yet. So, the big fat dick of the Turkish Army doesn't make him happy! Maybe it even hurts him, unlike the Syrian Army dick which is soft and thin and sensitive. Damn you, you intellectual with your puny choices from amongst a heap of pricks that has piled up in your rotten lap, looking to find one that's just right for your flabby anus.'

My uncle never talked like this, one obscenity after another. Not a string of obscenities, he never spoke like this. But what that writer put on his Facebook page demolished my uncle's self-control to the point that he was using words that probably wouldn't enter the mind of the dirtiest-talking sex worker.

'Alan, my nephew! Alan, my sister's son! Just listen up to what your uncle has to say. You can hate the Turk. That's your right. Maybe it's your duty. After all, the Turk has marinated you in the soup of oppression and suffering. But that doesn't mean that you go and welcome with open arms another someone who has been keeping you down for decades. And it doesn't mean you rejoice when you see people coming who have plundered your identity through many long years and have made you taste every brand of humiliation and abasement and tyranny and disgrace. It also doesn't mean that you celebrate the people who have prevented you from singing in your own language, even at mere weddings. Right—even with everything that has gone on, it doesn't mean you go and sing praises to this oppressor over here, and decide you prefer him over that other oppressor over there, and so you dance a jig for his pleasure and then you go on and strip off whatever rags you've still got covering your bare butt until you're as naked as any cheap whore standing out there on the street. This guy who wrote those stupid meaningless words is just a fucking prostitute, this guy sells his pen cheap.'

As my uncle was speaking, he was adding a red 'piss me off' emoji to the 'ratty little prostitute's' words. That was how he described it. Nothing would calm him down. He began pacing, and all morning long I could see the tension on his face. Sometime in the afternoon, he picked up his bouzouki and walked out.

'I might not come back tonight. Don't worry about me.'

***

I took advantage of my uncle's absence by going to Mazyat's house. I told my mother I was just going out for a short tour on Khadraa. On my dear green bike, I headed through the narrow lanes northward until I got to her house. As soon as I stepped inside, I felt the heat in the sitting room and took in the powerful scent that hung over everything. The TV was still blaring out the news of the warm welcome given by the crowds to the young and triumphant journalist when he reached the centre of Afrin City.

Mazyat didn't pay much attention to what was going on in the outside world. Like me, she saw and heard that the Syrian People's Army had arrived in Afrin to support the Kurdish People's Defense Units. But she wasn't interested. Switching off the TV and opening the doors to her wardrobe, she said, 'Kamo, my darling, your dick is more important to me than anything else. And not just for me—but for you, too. Believe me. All of this talk you're hearing and these reports they keep telling us about on the TV, none of it has any value compared to your dick.'

Mazyat was putting on some see-through underwear I hadn't

seen before. It was red, and it was made of a soft satiny material. In fact, what she was putting on that day was nothing more than a few threads that revealed more than they hid of her tasty body. She put these threads on and came toward me slowly, like a lioness gathering her forces to finish off a straying gazelle whose legs blind fate had driven into the ambush—a nice, freshwater spring—set for her.

She hissed as she bent down and pressed her bosom against my face. 'Don't forget that my crotch has as much value as your gorgeous dick, sweetheart.'

I put my arms around her. I slipped one hand down to her bottom and pressed my fingernails into her flesh.

'You've got to sow your seed inside me—tonight. I want to get pregnant from you. Got it? Do you understand what I'm saying?'

A Suicide

Sharraan?

'It means *battles*, Kamo.'

When my Uncle Ali the bouzouki player told me that the name of this village actually means *battles*, what popped into my head were my hot battles on Mazyat's wide bed. She hadn't said anything to me about what the name of this place—Sharraan, I mean—meant. She hadn't explained what her own name—Mazyat—meant, either. She didn't even ask me about the meaning of my name. She wasn't a woman driven by curiosity to stick her nose into questions of meaning, whether it was what the names of villages meant, or the names given to different places, or to people. Her attention was focused completely on one meaning, one sense of the way things were, and no other. On transforming the war into some sort of ultimate pleasure, whatever it would cost.

Many months passed after I got to know the beautiful Mazyat, during which she was completely obsessed by turning this war into a kind of pleasure.

But before another new year—2018, I mean—and in a way that seemed to be in cahoots with the threats from Turkey to attack Afrin District, something happened that would have been impossible to believe if it hadn't happened. Strong winds coming from the north set in, and the sky rained down red olives. They looked like huge carnelian beads.

'It's the end of the world! The Day of Judgment has come!' That's what people were shrieking, their faces in shock at the sight of red olives falling from the sky. There wasn't a single olive tree left standing that wasn't denuded, losing the leaves that clothed it in that storm raging from the north. Wherever you turned, you couldn't help seeing olive trees stripped bare except for their very, very dark-red olives. It was exactly like Mazyat pulling off her clothes in the bedroom on my visits to her.

This wasn't some ordinary event. The trees on both sides of the road made for a frightening scene, bearing olives the colour of blood. As we steered our bikes toward a nearby village, across an olive grove, my Uncle Ali shouted, 'But olive trees are always green. Stripped bare—this is totally strange, it's unbelievable.'

We went on for a few metres before he added, 'What's strangest of all are these bloody beads, olive-beads. They look exactly like drops of blood, hanging there on these olive trees. It doesn't make any sense at all. Olives can be dark green, they can be black, they can be dark brown. But this colour? Like blood? Makes no sense at all.'

***

Sharraan was a village surrounded by fields that seemed to go on endlessly, and all of them were planted thickly with olive trees. I would ride through them on my green bike, steering along the narrow lanes that separated one tree from another. But when the olives turned red and began to fall, I was afraid to go alone into those silent and gloomy groves. I began taking my brother Alan with me. I would put him on the back of the bike and we'd shoot from one field into the next.

One day when we were on the bike, Alan said he could hear crying and moaning coming from one of the groves. I stopped and listened. Everywhere, it was completely silent. There wasn't a sound except for the hiss of the wind as it curled around the branches of these endless, squat olive trees. But my brother was scared.

'What you're hearing is the wind, stupid', I said. 'Don't you know that the wind makes a sound that's like wailing?'

'It's the sound of crying.'

Alan went on insisting that he was right. His face was pale, and I stopped and set the bike down by the side of the lane. I took his hand and we headed for a nearby tree. Like all the other trees, it was dripping with red olives. When we got very close and stopped, we really did hear a sound like a woman crying. But there was no one here. As far as you could see, there were long parallel rows of trees, and they were all dripping with these blood-red olives. But there weren't any human beings anywhere nearby.

And then suddenly the whole grove of trees was alive with the sound of human sobbing. The trees were crying. All the trees were crying.

I got us out of that field fast, my heart pounding in terror. I put Alan on the back of the bike and headed for home without a look back and without taking any detours. I told my mother what we had heard, me and Alan. She didn't believe us. She pulled Alan to her chest and gave him a tight hug and began stroking his hair and kissing him and comforting him.

When my uncle came in, I told him, too. He looked sad but said nothing. He reached for the bouzouki and began playing some weepy melodies by the artist Ali Tijo, the kind that made my mother cry.

People were afraid. They were talking about the Turkish attack that everyone was expecting. Some people were packing their belongings, intending to flee to the city of Afrin. But the Party comrades forbade it, telling them not to believe the rumours. Nothing was going to happen. This was psychological warfare. Right here, in this town, we would stand and fight and resist any aggression.

I was afraid, too. Several times I really wanted to talk about it all with my uncle. But there was something that kept him from paying much attention to me. The only choice left for me was to go to the house of the widow Mazyat and tell her about the strange things that were happening in the town. I got on my bike and rode off furiously. I found the door to her house open. Cautiously, I went inside. I didn't hear any of the usual noise, none of the commotion I had always heard when I showed up here. Usually, I would hear her voice, humming the tune of one of Fairuz's songs or a melody by the Kurdish singer-songwriter Rojin, or some other song, as she was polishing kitchenware, straightening the lounge, or doing some other task.

My feet led me as usual to her bedroom, our warm and pretty den. And then the shock slammed into me. Mazyat was lying on her back, her bulging eyes staring at the ceiling. I could see blood all over; she seemed to be swimming in it. Scattered across her bed and all around it, everywhere, there were red olives, dripping blood.

I fled. No one saw me—there was no one anywhere who would have found me here. The streets were all empty. When I reached home, I found my mother crying.

'Why is mama crying?' I asked Alan, and he shrugged. From the next room, my uncle yelled out. 'Mazyat committed suicide. Do you know who I mean? The young widow, poor thing, the one your mother always went to visit.'

'Suicide?'

'Yes, Kamo. She killed herself. Don't you know that widows do that when there's a war going on?'

***

My uncle didn't tell me how he'd got the news of Mazyat's killing, or her *suicide,* as he called it. And I didn't ask him. And I certainly didn't tell anyone that I had seen her, drowning in her own blood with cursed red olives scattered all around her. I begged God that my mother wouldn't be widowed during this war. I begged God to keep my father alive even if he stayed a prisoner of Daesh from now until the Day of Judgment. Because of course he would return to his family one day, he must return. The important thing was that my mother not become a widow and commit suicide.

I couldn't sleep that night. I couldn't get the image of Mazyat sinking into her own blood out of my mind. When I imagined the scene, she was shivering, just like the branch of an olive tree thick with blood-olives.

For the next several days, I didn't leave the house at all. I heard from one of my uncle's phone conversations that conditions were very bad. I heard about the build-up of troops. Turkish units and the militias allied with them were massing all along the border, from Qastal Jindu to Sharraan and on to Atma, a bit further on from Rajo, a town near the border with Idlib Governorate.

Now, at the end of the year, many people were bundling up their possessions and preparing themselves to move on to the city of Afrin. My mother was one of them. She had a massive bag ready to go. She had already put some of our clothes in it and had set it down next to the front door.

The farmers, who had been on the point of beginning to pick their olives, abandoned the mats they used to cover the ground all around the trees, and the sticks they used to shake the higher branches so that the olives would fall to the ground. Instead, they got ready to leave their olive trees. They left everything as it was in the hope they would be coming back very soon. All they took with them were belongings that were valuable and didn't weigh much, as they set out in the direction of Afrin.

The growing season this year was different from the year before. Or rather, in the first place, there wasn't a 'season' this year, other than the season of tanks which swept across the olive groves, moving in every direction. Last year, my mother and Alan and I had gone to help with the olive harvest, and we got hourly pay for our work. It was really nice work to do and we had a good time doing it. First, we spread the mats out across the ground beneath the olive trees. Some of the men were already climbing up wooden ladders to shake the high branches and comb them with winnowing forks in order to get the olives to fall onto the mats. My work consisted entirely of picking the olives out of the leaves, which also fell, and separating the hard green olives from the ones that had already ripened. My mother and the other women were putting some of the olives in clear plastic bags to be sent to the souq in Afrin. The rest, the ripest ones, would be sent by the owner of the olive grove to the olive press, to be made into oil.

Our lives were pretty good, those days in the autumn of 2017.

Traveling musicians would come to us in the fields and play musical pieces that we enjoyed, or they would sing the songs of Jamil Horo and Ali Tijo and others, while we stood up and clustered around cheerfully, listening to the music. The musician wouldn't stop plucking, or blowing if he was playing a mizmar, or singing, until the olive-grove owner came over to him and gave him a bit of money or a sack of olives. Then he would go off to another spot. And there were the girls—they formed circles and danced dabkes after the day's harvesting was done and before the tractor or the pickup came to take us home after a day filled with happy moments.

Fuck the War.

It stole everything from me, even being able to enjoy the olive harvest. Even thinking about the woman who got me to enjoy life.

Safe Corridor

We fled from Sharraan before the armed groups who were flunkies for Turkey arrived. The image of Mazyat drowning in her own blood on a bed that had seen the happiest moments of my life fled along with me. Through all the difficult routes of our flight from Sharraan, as we made our way on foot to the city of Afrin, that painful scene would not leave my mind.

But I had new things to think about. Once we were in Afrin, it was only a few days before the city itself was surrounded. When we were under siege, the Turks announced that their army had opened a safe corridor for civilians to leave, a passage heading south.

'A safe corridor?' That's what Uncle Naaso barked, his voice full of scorn. He had us staying in his house in Afrin—that is, before we had to flee from there, too.

'If the Turks were to open a million safe corridors', he added, 'I wouldn't go. This is a crafty, underhanded plan to empty the city of everyone who lives here, so that only the fighters are left. Where are we supposed to go, anyway? Have we forgotten the people of Kobani and what happened to them once they left their homes? Have we forgotten the other civilians who have fled their homes in this war, and then have been imprisoned in migrant camps? Staying at home, dying at home—that's better than the humiliation of being a homeless vagrant.'

'But Uncle Naaso, we aren't alone. We aren't the only ones. Everyone is going to leave as soon as things quiet down a little.

Whenever the bombing stops, people are ready to leave. Can't you hear the missiles? They're exploding in every street.'

'I can hear them. How could I not hear them? Am I deaf? But I won't run away no matter what happens. And you're welcome to stay here with me, here in my house. You're my guests in any case, whatever happens.'

The man we called Uncle Naaso—he wasn't our real uncle, but we called him that out of respect—refused to evacuate, refused heatedly and with utter stubbornness. That is, until a missile fell on the garage directly opposite the building where he lived.

'The bastards are going to kill us. Okay, it looks like you're right. Let's go.'

We all hurried down to the street. In the lead were Uncle Naaso's family. My mother came down with her arms wrapped around her enormous bag of clothing and such. Uncle Ali was cradling his bouzouki and scowling. Alan was dragging his feet. I felt like I was about to vomit though I didn't know why.

Uncle Naaso brought his farm tractor around to where we were standing. We climbed into the trailer and set off right away. Only a few minutes later, the tractor was stopped by the unimaginably large crowds of people who were blocking the way. The pause lasted about a quarter of an hour and in that time the trailer filled up with other people. There must have been more than twenty of them, women and children and an elderly man with his injured son, as he explained to my uncle when he asked my uncle and some other men to help him out. My uncle didn't say a word. He twisted to look back and stared sadly at this man and his son who was wrapped up in a red and white blanket, and he gazed at all of these other evacuees whom he had never seen before in his life. Then he turned around and began driving. We were going east. In half an hour, we had crossed the Afrin River. He turned south, toward Turindah. This was the road the Turks had announced as a safe route for the evacuation of civilians fleeing the whippings of the Zeytin Dalı: the so-called Turkish 'Olive Branch', its army operation in northeast Syria.

During the first hour, I was standing up, facing the cold breezes and letting them strike my face as I gripped the side wall of the trailer and stared out at the sad, gloomy, weary-looking olive groves. I stared in bewilderment at these crowds of people escaping the city of Afrin and its surrounding villages. Refugees, as far as you could see. One caravan of vehicles was followed without a break by another—farm tractors, pickups, cars, motorbikes, little carts and microbuses all crowding in to join the uneven lanes of traffic that were moving extremely slowly. At the side of the road, I saw lots and lots of people who hadn't been able to find a spot in any vehicle and were evacuating on foot. I saw women dragging little children while balancing huge sacks on their heads; teenagers holding the hands of elderly people with white plastic rubbish bags slung over their shoulders that held blankets and clothing. Everyone was walking in silence, as if they had all been struck dumb like my mother.

When we got close to the village of Turindah, the moaning stopped. The moaning of the wounded boy wrapped up in the blood-stained blanket. One of the old women said to his father, 'It looks like your son has gone to sleep. That's good. That means he'll get better.' I was still standing up, watching the endless caravan with a whole crowd of images going through my head. When I heard the elderly women speaking to the old man after his son had gone quiet, I stepped down and sat on the trailer floor, watching this scene in front of me. I saw the man bend over his son, putting his head down over his boy's heart and then gripping his wrist. Moments later, he was staring up into the sky. The look on his face was all anger, grief, and confusion. I was completely riveted by his face. His features were hard, sharp in fact, even though he was so old. He put one hand up to his head which was covered in a red shimagh. His other hand was searching for something in his vest pocket. I kept my eyes on him, studying every move. His face had just been raided by a vicious, deep anger and infinite bewilderment. He pulled his pack of cigarettes from his pocket, drew one out, and lit it. He blew the smoke upward into the sky covered in dark clouds. Then he turned to my Uncle Ali and to Uncle Naaso.

'Please, help me down, with my son here.' His voice was full of grief.

Uncle Naaso turned to look at him. 'Why, brother? Stay with us. We'll make the trip, we'll get there.'

'My trip ends here. My boy dying has ended it. Please let me get out.'

The women shouted in unison. 'He's dead?'

'Yes. He's dead. All his blood has haemorrhaged. Please, let me out. At least I can go back to my village to bury him there.' The old man's voice told me he was in utter despair. Despite the attempts of Uncle Naaso and my Uncle Ali, and the imploring voices of the women sitting in the tractor trailer, the man wouldn't budge from his request to get out with his son's body.

There was nothing that Uncle Naaso and my Uncle Ali could do but climb out of the tractor, take the boy's body from his father's arms, and lay it out on the roadside. They helped the old man down from the tractor trailer and stood there with him, consoling him and urging him over and over to get back in and go on with his journey. But the man just went on insisting he would stay with his son and return to their village to bury him.

'I'll put the boy to rest in the village. It isn't very far from here. Even if I have to carry him on my back, I'm taking him to the village. I'll bury him next to our dead, near the olive grove. I'll take him there even if a sniper hunts me on the way there. My son chose to die as we were trying to leave—leaving our home. That is the hardest thing to do in this cursed war. In wars, people live on because they can't meet the high costs of dying. Go on, now—go on your way. Leave me here with my son. Leave me here, please, I beg you. My dead son will not have to taste the humiliation of being a refugee, no matter what happens now.'

By now, the man's tone wasn't so much sad as it was angry—and also, shot through with resignation. But Uncle Naaso was determined not to abandon the old man.

'How can we leave you here and go off? It's not possible—'

But this was the moment when the long line of vehicles began to move again. The driver of the car behind our tractor grumbled loudly about how long he had already waited for the queue to start up again. He put his head out the window and began shouting.

'Hey there, folks, hurry up, finish your talking there so we can get going and get there. I have women and children and sick people with me. This tractor of yours is blocking the road. We're not out here for a little trip to the park. Behind me are hundreds of cars and trucks carrying families who are evacuating, leaving their homes, and they've been waiting to get there.'

But—to get where? No one could say what their destination actually was. The end point changed from one minute to the next. We will go to Aleppo. No, we will go to the town of Nubbul. No—we'll go the other way, we'll go back. No—we'll camp here in the fields and orchards until hopefully everything calms down. No—there will be camps ready, waiting for us, there. The comrades must have arranged things for us, they must know what they're doing.

The sound of a car horn. The car of the man who wouldn't stop shouting as he waved his hand, telling us to get going. Move it! That was followed by the sounds of other car horns, coming from the vehicles that were stopped behind him. Uncle Naaso had no choice. He had to start driving in order to clear the way for all these other people.

I watched as he said goodbye to the old man with obvious warmth, and Uncle Ali did, too. The poor man stayed where he was, by the side of the road with his son's body, his bundle in one hand and his other hand shoved into his pocket, staring in total bewilderment at the blanket that was still wrapped around the body of his son, who only a few minutes before had been moaning.

'What a terrible, sad scene,' I said to my uncle. He was climbing into his seat next to Uncle Naaso.

'Sadness, in situations like this, is useless,' he said. 'It doesn't mean anything.' Uncle Naaso said nothing. He just gripped the steering column hard and drove, following the vehicle ahead of us.

Uncle Naaso

He's a good man, al-Khal Naaso, sweet and tender to others, and always merry. I don't think I ever saw him without a smile on his face. Even in the most devastating moments of the bombing, he managed to spread a feeling of joy amongst us and to lift off our fear and anxiety. One time, when the airplanes were circling around up there, seeming to hover exactly over our heads and then erupting with truly terrifying sounds, he poked his middle finger at them and spoke in anger. 'Raise as much of a ruckus as you want, you whores. In the end, your fate is to fall onto Kamiran's cock.'

When I heard him say this, I felt very embarrassed and dropped my head. Uncle Naaso gave me a look and began laughing. 'Don't be ashamed, boy,' he teased me. 'War is just a big huge eraser. It wipes out all the shame and embarrassment.'

I smiled, imagining a tank coming behind us in the shape of a gigantic eraser and uprooting the olive trees planted in such even rows on either side of this safe corridor—such straight rows that they reminded me of the lines written out in one of my father's letters, the ones I had written in my own hand.

I was remembering you, too, my pretty chalk, my fantastic beautiful pale little friend. I said to myself, I will use my chalk to draw a tank facing off against an olive tree. I'll draw a whole battle, from my imagination, a battle between a tank shaped like an eraser and an olive tree in the shape of a word. With this drawing of mine, I can show how the word stands firm as it faces the tank.

So, as we were having a rest period that we didn't have any choice about, since we were stopped at the crush of cars and trucks and the enormous long queue of people evacuating, which went on for more than an hour, I began searching for something I could use for my sketch, this picture I had drawn in my head. I couldn't find anything to use except some thin scrappy torn rags and piles of shit that seemed to be everywhere along this part of the route.

The odour of shit hung in the air along the whole evacuation route. I never understood where it all came from. Were the airplanes that were sent out as part of the Olive Branch military campaign against the Kurdish areas strafing the whole area with shit? Or was it the armed men of the attacking units and the soldiers in the Turkish Army? Maybe they were planting shit instead of sinking their mines in the earth.

Al-Khal Naaso watched as I wandered around at the side of the road. He laughed. 'What are you looking for, Kamo?'

'I want to draw.'

'Draw?'

'Yes.'

'So, what do you want to draw?'

'A tank. An eraser. An olive tree. A word.'

Uncle Naaso chuckled, and then he roared so hard that the olive branches all around trembled. He was still chortling when he spoke again. 'You want to draw what's in my mind? Isn't that it, thief?!'

Before I could answer him 'yes', he jabbed his finger towards the mounds of shit that sat piled alongside the masses of evacuees. 'Draw the shit, my boy. This is the reality of war in this country of ours. Draw a huge mountain of shit with green horseflies in the air above it. It's only shit that can really express this ukht sharmuta war, this sister-of-a-whore war. The warplane making all that noise is just a side issue, a mere detail. The whoretank is another minor detail.'

'Minor detail? What does that mean?'

'It means, Kamo my boy, it means war isn't just a tank that's firing at you or an airplane attacking you. You can call these things *the appearances war makes*, or *the way war looks*. But war itself is something else. It might be hard for me to really explain it to you right now. Because I've got something urgent I have to take care of. Your Uncle Ali knows how to drive the tractor and he'll do the rest of this refugee journey with you. He might also explain the rest of it, too. Because I have to go back to Afrin.'

'Go back? When the whole world is trying to escape?'

'Yes, go back. I will go back and stay there, to stay beside the statue of Kawa. How could it have slipped our minds that we were abandoning him, leaving him there all alone? They will shatter him to pieces. I know that. I've been a soldier and I know exactly what it means to carry a weapon on your shoulder. All you need is a gun in your hand for your brain to shrink and descend into the lowest of the low. I know what will happen, I know those soldiers full of hate will piss all over him. And if they do, we won't be able to wash away that stain on our honour. Ever. I know it. I know it very well.'

'But—'

Uncle Naaso didn't give me a chance to say what I was thinking, to object to what he was doing. He didn't even wait for me to finish my sentence. He cut it off with a sweep of his hand, as if he were erasing something from an invisible slate. He left me very quickly. He left the spot where we were stopped without even giving me the chance to lean over, lowering my head to kiss his hand as we children always do when we say goodbye to older men, or when we say hello to them. His family were all fast asleep. He didn't even go over to give them a final look or a goodbye before he walked away.

***

Al-Khal Naaso's house was near the garage where the buses parked, at the Kawa al-Haddad roundabout. He had different varieties of flowers around his sitting room, which was spacious and airy, and he had more flowers sitting on his balcony overlooking the road. From that balcony, we could see the roundabout. We could watch the yellow taxis and see the shops, and above all we could see the huge statue of Kawa the legendary blacksmith hero, whose fire led the Kurds to freedom thousands of years ago.

'As long as Kawa is standing there where he belongs,' Uncle Naaso always said, 'nothing will happen to Afrin.'

We lived in Uncle Naaso's house for about a week. Every evening, he joked with us. Once, with a smile, he even said, glancing toward my Uncle Ali, 'You abandoned Sharraan and fled! You left it for the jackals who will strip it clean and you came to live in Afrin as evacuees? What a dishonour! Shameful!'

My mother, who was submerged in her silence as she always was, said nothing to that. But my Uncle Ali, who knew that these words were meant for him, obviously objected and showed it in his expression.

'Uncle Naasan', he said—and I noticed he used Uncle Naaso's formal name—we fled because we are civilians. The comrades were defending the place, and a lot of them were martyred. Do you want me to count them for you?'

'I'm joking, Ali. I don't want you to count the martyrs. I know what's happening better than you do. I know that Afrin was sold off to the Turks because of the Russians and the Americans. I know that they exchanged Afrin for the Ghouta. The war in Syria, these days, is just one gigantic bazaar. And I know that the blood of our martyrs is the cheapest merchandise in the bazaar of politics. I only said what I said because I'm so angry and so beaten down. Believe me. Believe me, nephew. Inside, I'm boiling like a big pot and the fire beneath the pot never dies down.'

***

A light rain began falling the instant Uncle Naaso left us. I watched him go. On the damp ground, his steps made olive tree patterns. Yes. Every step Uncle Naaso took left behind it the imprint of an olive tree. The sight bewildered me, and I called out to Uncle Ali. From the tone of my voice, he could tell I was afraid.

'Uncle, do you see what I see?'

'This is just Uncle Naaso. His footsteps are the shape of little olive trees, Kamiran. What's strange about that?'

'It's strange.'

'What's strange, Kamo?'

'The olive trees, Uncle.'

'Hey, my little donkey. When were olive trees something strange in Afrin?'

Uncle Naaso was further away from the convoy by now, going in the opposite direction from where we were supposed to be going. His cigarette in his mouth, he was blowing smoke at the airplanes that were making a racket in the sky overhead. They were flying over the whole area. Then I noticed that the olive-tree shapes that I had seen in the mud as he walked away were rising straight up. They were turning into trees. After every step that left behind the image of an olive sapling, there was a tree shooting up from the ground. It was astonishing. It seemed my uncle was following this, too, and looking at the same spots where I was looking.

'Ya ilahi!!' shouted my Uncle Ali as he watched this supernatural scene taking place. At that point, we hadn't gotten very far from the village of Turindah. In fact, the houses in the village were still visible through the drizzle. They looked sad and dejected.

Suddenly we heard the sound of a sniper's bullet. A single shot. *In my head I sketched a picture frame of moans, and an orphan bullet sketched a shadow for the tree of death.* That's what my uncle chanted after the terrible scene was over.

Uncle Naaso fell to the ground like an ancient olive tree attacked by an army of hoes. He fell to the ground like the statue of Kawa al-Haddad at the bus garage near his home. In those same seconds, I saw the olive trees on either side of the road where Uncle Naaso fell topple just as he had. The trees were all moaning and the sound went on and on. I listened hard for about a quarter of an hour as the little olive trees groaned. I didn't have any doubt that they were crying. I went up to one olive tree at the roadside and touched its decrepit trunk. I put my ear down against it. The tree trunk really was giving off a low moan, like the sound of a little child who is suffocating.

I was afraid.

I was very afraid, and I stepped back. Way back.

Al-Khal Naaso's corpse was still there on the ground. It wasn't far away, but we didn't dare come any closer.

'What are you doing, stupid?'

'I'm trying to hear the olive trees crying.'

The rain stopped and the air cleared. You could see thousands of olive trees washed by the rain, all leaning so far over that they looked as if they were about to fall.

'Look, Uncle,' I said. 'The trees, they're tipping over.'

Uncle Ali didn't even glance in the direction I was waving. 'Don't you know, Kamo, that olive trees are very sensitive plants? Yes, they're sensitive, they feel things. If they lose their owner they kill themselves. The olive trees are committing suicide, Kamiran. Right now, right here, they're committing suicide.'

I walked away from my uncle, going a few steps toward the body of Uncle Naaso which was stretched out on the ground. Over there. Now, it looked like he was somewhere a bit further away than he had been.

'They'll shoot you, donkey. Come back up here. You can't go any closer. C'mon, get in.'

Would they really have shot their sniper bullets into us if we had gone back to take the body? I don't know.

'Going back' meant only one thing: 'Going back to Afrin.' And going back to Afrin had become *impossible, for now the sniper draws the frame with his bullets.* That was my uncle again. What he said didn't make a lot of sense to me. Then he gave me something of an explanation.

'What I mean is, the sniper plays the tune of treachery on the strings of his gun.'

But that just made everything my uncle had said even harder to understand. I kept after him, asking him stubbornly to tell me what he meant. 'So, who is this sniper you're talking about, Uncle?'

'The sniper is the haziness of death in the clarity of war.'

'What does that mean?!'

'It means: Go and take your seat in the trailer next to your mother and don't distract me any more from driving this tractor. Got it?'

'Got it.'

That's what I said to my uncle when I could see he was getting really irritated. And also, I could feel the seriousness in his words. I got up from where I was sitting next to him and went and climbed into the back, standing up as I had done before.

***

I wonder, would the olive trees have planted themselves there like that in the wake of our footsteps, if we had turned back and killed the sniper like he killed Uncle Naaso?

I don't know.

And I don't know who dragged away Uncle Naaso's body. Or where they buried it. I don't know whether the old man got back to his village and buried his son or whether he stayed there at the side of the road guarding his son who was lying there wrapped up in a blanket.

What I do know is that we went on our way, moving forward very slowly. Uncle Ali drove the tractor pretty carelessly. When I got tired of standing, and of seeing these repeated images of evacuees walking along the road, I went and sat down next to my mother. It seemed to be the same scene repeating itself, over and over, all up and down this route for many kilometres. I gripped my uncle's bouzouki and amused myself by plucking at the strings in a way that made my mother laugh. But soon my uncle shouted, 'Leave the bouzouki alone, Kamiran! You've fucked the strings.'

'You're just about fucking the tractor, uncle,' I responded, jumping up. But he didn't hear the sarcasm in my voice because the tractor motor and the creaking sounds coming from the trailer were so loud.

***

What does it mean, *safe corridor*?

I don't know what devil whispered in my brother Alan's ear that he should put this question to me while we were stopped next to another olive grove to get some sleep.

I didn't think about it for very long before answering him. 'Do you remember the old man in the red shimagh whose son died here, right here in this tractor-trailer?'

'Yes.'

'Do you remember Uncle Naaso who was killed by some sniper's bullet but we don't know who it was?'

'Yes.'

'Do you remember the shit you stepped in several times during the day when we were sleeping in the trailer for two nights trying to keep ourselves warm enough in a stupid thin nylon blanket?'

'Uh, yes?'

'Do you remember the heavy rain that swept away your shit? Do you remember the war planes that were always up there in the sky in a total free-for-all? Do you remember the olive groves we left behind? Remember the women crying as they got into the buses? The children crying? Did you see how many fleeing people were sinking into the mud and trying to protect themselves from the rain by crouching under the olive trees on the road from Afrin to here? Do you—'

'Yes yes yes. I'm not so little, Kamo,' Alan said impatiently. 'I remember everything. Just like you. And anyway, it's only been a few hours since any of that happened, not long enough for me to forget. Just answer my question: What is this safe corridor?'

My voice was even. 'Safe corridor, Alan—it's all of these things I just said and it's also other disasters, ones I didn't mention. Safe corridor means everything except actually being safe. Just this one tractor trailer has seen two awful things happen: Uncle Naaso being killed by a sniper and the death of that boy who didn't stop moaning until he died, because his wound was hurting so much. So now, just imagine the thousands of tractors and buses and taxis out there. Thousands of stories and probably more terrible than the stories we've seen in the trailer of Uncle Naaso's tractor. Do you see all those totally confused people out there? Do you see Uncle Naaso's family members, who are still sleeping and don't even know what happened? Do you see these cars lined up behind us? Every man and woman in every car is a story on their own. Every car and every truck hides tragedies and painful stories, as many of them as there are people inside. The safe corridor, what it is—it's the fear of never getting there. And it's not knowing in the first place where you're headed, anyway.'

I don't know if Alan was convinced by my answer. But he got up and went and pressed his cheek against the cold edge of the trailer wall, as the tractor now headed for the village of Basuta. Then he stared out at the side of the road, which was completely choked with the file of evacuees walking, walking, as far as you could see.

I was very tired. I needed some sleep. I curled up at my mother's feet as she sat listening to the women telling their stories. I put my head in my mother's lap and closed my eyes, hoping I would be lucky enough to get a little share of sleep.

Zallukh

The tractor came to a stop at an olive grove. The tractor that was pulling all of us—me, my uncle and mother and Alan and some of the others who were fleeing, including the strange old woman Zallukh from a village in Badina. We didn't know why the tractor was stopping this time. But we had gotten used to frequent stops, ever since we'd left Afrin. The line of cars and jeeps and trucks was always very, very long and the road was narrow, so of course there was a lot of stopping.

No one will believe—not even you, my beloved chalk, my Safra—what I'm going to tell you about this old woman from one of the hamlets of Badina, which is to the southeast of Rajo. According to the people who were with her, this old woman lived through the occupation of Rajo and Badina and the little enclaves around them. They came under occupation on the third of March.

Zallukh was a simple woman, and she was a widow. She had a low stone house on the slope of Jabal Bilink—Tiger Mountain—and about a hundred olive trees, a small grove that gave her enough to live on. She had lived alone in that little house ever since her sons had gone to Europe, all of them, and there was nobody left to care for her except a young widow whose husband, a fighter with the People's Defence Units in Raqqa, had been killed in the skirmishes with Daesh.

This old woman had witnessed the advance of the Turkish Army and the units loyal to it toward her village. She said to herself, 'Why should I flee? I'm an old widow and nobody pays attention to widows when a war is going on. So, I will just stay in my village, not try to escape. I'll keep watch over my olive trees and stay with them no matter what.'

These were the words she repeated to us. And she added, 'I stayed in my house even though the airplanes were roaring overhead and I could hear the big guns. But what gave me a surprise one day was a very loud explosion, boom boom! It sounded like it was next door. I went outside to see what it was, and I saw two armed men with long black beards and hair—God preserve us—

'"What do you want?" I asked them.

'One of them said, "We want you to leave your house and go away. The war is on and you have to go somewhere safe."

'"There's no place in the world safer than my home."

'"Ya Khala," the other man said. "We're telling you to leave. This is an order and you have to follow it. Leave means leave."'

She sighed. 'There was no one anywhere in sight to defend me right then. Everyone had left me. I was alone, like an old worn-out olive tree on the summit of Jabal Bilink. I was afraid for my life. Iyy wAllahi, I was! Why should I lie? Life, one's soul ... it's precious. I was afraid of them. That's why I said to them, "I'll leave. But on one condition. I take with me a handful of olives I'll pick from my little olive grove here." They agreed. Why wouldn't they agree? I went to the olive trees, and they went with me. The two of them polluted my little grove. I didn't want to leave it. I pulled off the first olive and I held it as tightly as if I was trying to hold on to my soul.

'"Hurry up, Khala." That was those men again, trying to get me out of the olive grove I worked so hard on for years and years, working and watering and tending. I planted the seedlings before those two men with their weapons were even born. Akhkh … akhkh. I picked two more olives. I had the feeling those little olives wanted me to save them. All the little trees, the whole field, everything was begging me to save them all. All the fields of Afrin were begging to be saved, they were afraid of being violated.

'"Hurry up or we'll drag you out of this field. We don't have the time to waste here with you."

'They hurried me up all right—they hurried me to my death. They hurried me to abandoning the precious core of my soul, that olive grove, to going away. I picked a few more olives. I stood there crying under a healthy, flourishing olive tree that was a memorial from my dear late husband. He planted it with his own hands before he died, and he charged me with tending it well. Every olive tree in my field has a story. If I were to tell them all, I would still be telling stories a year from now. Those two men with their guns didn't know the stories of those trees. The only thing that mattered to them was getting me to empty my house and my field for them. Those two men with their guns didn't care about my grief. They attacked me and they dragged me and then they threw me outside the field. I was afraid they were going to grab the handful of olives I had. All I could do was to tighten my fist. Then I went away. My heart, my goodness, it was ripping to shreds with the pain of it. Those armed units stole the olive presses, one after another, they ransacked them. They stole thousands of jerry cans full of oil. I saw them carrying these things off to the trailers attached to tractors and cars that they had stolen from their owners. They burned all the fields. I heard the keening of the oil in those trees with my own ears. Have you ever heard the sound of olive oil moaning? Yes, that's right, my children—olive oil makes a sound as piercing and shiny as gold.'

'Auntie Zallukh is raving', my uncle said. 'There's nothing more silent than oil. Even when we're pouring it into a bowl, it doesn't make a sound, because it's so thick.'

'But when we fry potatoes in it, or anything else, it makes a lot of noise,' I said, as if I had just announced an important discovery.

My uncle turned to look at me. He raised his right hand sharply from the steering column and waved it back and forth as if he wanted to slap me. But instead, he mussed up my hair. 'What you hear, you little rascal, is the sound made by whatever's cooking in the oil. It's not the sound of the oil itself.'

'So, Auntie Zallukh is lying?'

'No. She's not lying. Oil does have a voice that's like gold, as she said. This is completely true.'

'How?'

My uncle was gripping the steering column with both hands, and he sounded grumpy when he answered. 'When are you ever going to stop chattering, Kamo?'

'When the airplanes stop chattering, uncle.'

'The f-ing airplanes aren't encountering any ground-to-air missiles like your dick that would silence them. As for you, you chattery little nightingale, I will silence you, and I don't need any missiles to do it. From now on, I don't want to hear a word from you. Understand? Let me drive the tractor to its goal. Just leave me alone to do that and nothing else.'

'In fact, I really haven't understood, uncle. But you can consider it as understood. Tell me, though, please, what is this goal your tractor has?'

'The goal this tractor has is to shit on this war. Say to me once more *I really haven't understood*, and I'll make you understand some other way. Got it now?'

I could see this was no longer a joking matter. He was beginning to get aggressive, and he was losing his patience with me.

'Yes, I've understood now, Uncle. I understand very well.'

***

Amma Zallukh sat down in the back of the trailer, silent and sad, after she had finished telling her story and the story of how her little grove was stolen from her. I looked back at her now and then, feeling sorry for her. The tractor was only inching along because the road was so congested with the endless line of evacuees. The drizzle went on and on, and the drone of the motor went on and on, too, as we moved slowly along the narrow dirt road.

After a few hundred metres, though, the tractor came to an actual stop. And when I happened to glance back at the trailer, I got a surprise. It was a strange sight. Amma Zallukh's skin was slowly turning green. I looked at her wrinkled face and saw that it was already completely green. Soon her hands went green, too, and then her clothes, and then her watery eyes.

Even her tears were green. They looked like two very soft, ripe olives.

I was scared. My uneasiness made its way to my uncle. He made a sort of chuckling sound. 'Look at the sky,' he said.

Oh no—this was terrible to see. The sky was green—as green as if it had just turned itself into a football field. Then we saw Amma Zallukh trying to climb down from the crowded tractor trailer. We saw her blow up like a big balloon. Honestly, I saw it with my own eyes—I saw her turn into an egg-shaped mass that looked just like a giant olive.

Old Zallukh, from a village in Badina, turned into a great big olive. She became a dark green ball, and she rolled across the ground like a huge American football, after she'd rolled over and fallen out of the trailer while everyone watched, utterly dumbfounded and terrified.

Ferial the Yazidi

Ferial was a young Yazidi woman from the village of Qastal Jindu. I learned this as I was trying to get some sleep in the tractor trailer that my uncle had been driving ever since Uncle Naaso's murder. Ferial was recounting her ordeal to two old women who were wrapped up in heavy Turkish-made blankets.

'Ever since the Free Army took over the city of Izaz, six years ago, what ruled everyone in Qastal Jindo and the villages nearby was pure fear. I had just graduated from the College of Law in Aleppo.'

'Did you stay in the village, dear girl?' It was one of the old women, who was yawning.

'I'll tell you the whole story, Khala. We started to feel afraid—really afraid—that we would be a target for these Islamist militias who were with the Free Army, or whatever it was called after that. Some elements from these militias were coming into the village and telling us, "You are infidels, and you have to become Muslims." But they left us alone after that, so we didn't abandon the village. But the men and boys began carrying arms in case they had to block an attack on the village. Then a Kurdish People's Defence Unit was formed. So, we didn't try to evacuate. We stayed in our homes.'

'Alhamdulillah. You did better by staying there, in your village.'

'But then Daesh went into Izaz.'

'May God's curses come down on Daesh! God's curses on Daesh—

they've ruined homes and families everywhere,' exclaimed the other old woman, interrupting Ferial while still yawning. Ferial smiled. I looked sideways at my mother, and I could see that she was listening to Ferial's story and that she felt sad about it. Her face told me she was eager to hear the rest, though. I felt just as keen as she did to hear it. In fact, I was so eager that I could barely keep myself from looking up, straight at them, and saying to the two old women, 'Please, would you stop interrupting the young lady. Anyway, you need to go to sleep more than you need to hear more stories.' What I did instead was to close my eyes and sink into the pleasure of listening to the story that the two old women kept interrupting.

'I'm not going to give you a big painful headache with my story. I'll be quick with it. The Daesh elements attacked our village and the village of Qatma, too. They were trying to occupy both with their army.'

'Did they get into the village?'

'No. But there were a lot of manoeuvres and skirmishes, and bullets were fired by both sides. A lot of the teenaged boys and young men from the village joined up with the People's Defence Units. My fiancé Jaafar was one of them.'

'What's your name, my girl?'

'My name is Ferial. I used to be a lawyer, and—.'

One of the old women interrupted her. 'Is your fiancé still with them?' I didn't know which woman was speaking, but I could tell from the tone of her voice that she was yawning again. Out of sheer exhaustion, I figured. Miss Ferial spoke again, gently and sadly.

'Ya Khala, I'll tell you the whole story. Just give me a little time to say what I have to say.'

'If only these two old ladies were mutes instead of my mother the Arabic teacher,' I said to myself. 'If this were a conversation between Ferial and my mother, it would have a different flavour, for sure.' Opening my eyes again, I noticed what a strong interest my silent mother was clearly taking in Ferial's story. My mother's head was jutting forward, and she was supporting her dejected face on her right palm. In her features I could tell that she was anxious to talk with Ferial—now that she had learned about Ferial being a student in the College of Law in Aleppo.

As for the two old women, the pair gave into their drowsiness, both of them leaning back against the metal wall of the trailer and dropping off to sleep. Ferial the lawyer continued telling her story calmly. I'll call her *the lawyer*. I had no idea whether she had actually worked as a lawyer. But she had graduated from university, at least that's what she said. So, she was a lawyer. She was gazing at my mother.

'My fiancé was in combat against Daesh and he was martyred at the front, at Yazi Bagh, near the crossing into Turkey. I grieved so much for him. We were planning to get married at the New Year—less than a month after he was killed. Anyway, he sacrificed himself like so many hundreds of others. He was buried along with a whole party of martyrs in the Martyr Rafiq Cemetery in the village of Metina. After he died, we fled to the village of Qatma, nearby. We stayed there until Daesh left Izaz. But things didn't really improve. We were living daily terror—going to sleep in fear and waking up to it. In the shadow of this terrible fear, I got married. If only I hadn't. Two days before the sweep that destroyed everything, my husband went to Rajo to collect his payment for some loans he had made. I begged him not to go.

"The war's everywhere", I said to him, "and the wolves have bared their fangs even while they're waving olive branches." But he didn't listen to me. And ever since the destruction started, we haven't had any news of him at all. Did they lock him up? Did they kill him? Did he flee to some other place? I don't know anything. In a nutshell, we fled, again, to Qatma. Two days later, they occupied Qastal Jindu. Then the bombs caught up with us in Qatma, too. We took just a few clothes and blankets and fled to some relatives of ours in Qibar in the northern part of Afrin District. From Afrin, sister, you know the rest of the story.'

My mother responded with two big tears. Ferial the lawyer looked at her sadly, and added, 'Pardon me, sister. I'm very sorry, it looks like I've stirred up some pain. I haven't even asked your name.'

'Her name is Layla. She's my mother. And she can't speak.'

My words had an immediate impact on the lawyer. Sorrow welled up from her black eyes. She handed my mother a handkerchief and got up slowly. When I saw her standing, I could see how big and round her belly was. So, she was pregnant. 'That's all we need, in this safe corridor!' I said to myself. Then I was hit by a surging wave of sleepiness and I dozed off.

My Green Bicycle

There I was, racing my green bicycle along a dirt lane lined on both sides with white poplar trees so tall they almost blocked out the sky. I was in seventh heaven, going faster and faster until I had the sensation of taking off into the air. Suddenly a barrier appeared in front of me, with armed men clustered around it. A checkpoint. I couldn't go back, I couldn't escape. When I got closer, I could see the Turkish flag fluttering next to the flag of the Syrian Revolution. I breathed a sigh of relief. 'Alhamdulillah', I said to myself. 'It isn't a Daesh checkpoint. And I'm just a kid, they'll let me pass without any problem.'

Before I got to the barrier, though, I had such an urge to pee that I couldn't ignore it. What should I do? I couldn't decide. Should I stop and pee, and then go ahead to the checkpoint? Or keep going until I got there and ask the men there for permission to do it?

Suddenly I heard a rough voice ordering me to halt. 'Stop right there!'

I stopped right there.

I was pretty close by now to the huge barrels that formed the barricade. They were painted the colours of the Syrian Revolution flag. I could hear a Turkish song coming from a little shelter inside the checkpoint, blending in with the roar of the planes high above us.

A man was standing there in front of me. He wore a thick beard and army camouflage. He grabbed my handlebars.

‘Where did you steal this bike?’ His voice was harsh.

‘I didn’t steal it. It’s mine. My father bought it for me.’

‘Your father be damned, bloody liar. This bike belongs to my son Hamza.’ He began slapping me, hitting my body so hard that I was terrified. I started to pee.

***

I opened my eyes. I was still here in the trailer. So, what I had just seen was only a nightmare, nothing more. Like all the other nightmares I had during the nights. Ferial was pacing up and down in the trailer. The family of Uncle Naaso and the two old women were still fast sleep. My mother was sleeping, too. I stuck my hand inside my jeans, reaching for the space between my thighs. My underwear was soaked. I made sure that everyone was really asleep, but I still didn’t want to stand up. Ferial would find me out, and rascally Alan would, too. Even my uncle would see what was going on if he called me forward to the tractor. What should I do?! My secret, which I had been hiding for years now, would be revealed by this godawful nightmare in this cursed tractor trailer.

‘Alan!’

‘Yes, Kamo? Did you wake up?’

‘No-o-o… I’m still asleep.’

‘What do you want?’

‘I’m thirsty. Give me the water jug that’s sitting over there next to you.’

Alan crawled away from the side of the trailer and edged down towards me holding the jug. I took it from him and pretended to drink some water. Then I spilled it all over my jeans and began cursing my luck in a loud voice. The water mixed with the abominable pee. My little plan had worked. I handed the jug back to Alan and spoke in a whisper so that Ferial the lawyer wouldn't hear me.

'Fuck the safe corridor', I said.

Qafila: A Caravan Birth

When we arrived at Basuta, we slept one night in the pomegranate fields near some rocky hills to the east of town. We were: me, my mother and Alan, the lawyer Ferial, the two old women, and the family of Uncle Naaso who had slept the entire time, lying down or sitting up in the trailer pulled by the tractor that my Uncle Ali was driving, always slowly. We were piled up in that trailer like a slew of kittens or baby mice. Because there was so little space, we were knocked and tossed against each other, our bodies colliding as the tractor bumped along. As I sat in the trailer of that orange tractor, nothing bothered me as much as the piercing smell of people farting. One fart after another as the hours stretched on.

'The war is one big fart.' That's what I said to my uncle as we were waiting for the caravan of vehicles to move again, toward the village of Kimar.

When I turned my face away to avoid being infected by this stinky contagion, I felt a strong pinch. It was my mother. It seemed that the state of Ferial's belly had drawn her attention, too. I was used to getting these pinches from my mother, ever since she'd been stricken with muteness. She had begun pinching me as her way of asking me about something. A pinch always meant a question was coming.

'What do you want?' I asked her, my voice a little rough. My mother placed her hand level with her breasts and drew an upside-down arc in the air, with its lowest point below her navel. Then she looked at the pregnant lawyer and made a sign with her fingers, as if she were counting something. I understood that she wanted to know what month Ferial had gotten pregnant.

Ferial the lawyer was completely focused on picking the deep-red seeds out of a large pomegranate. Probably she had picked the fruit in the field by which we had parked to spend the night. She bit into the seeds, which were full of juice, with a peculiar kind of eagerness. I could see her soft face muscles tensing every time she took a bite, which meant the pomegranate seeds must be tart. I learned later, when I asked my Uncle Ali about it, that some pomegranates stay on their branches until the very end of winter if no one picks them earlier.

I was really put out by my mother's request! How was I going to ask this lady what month her pregnancy happened in? Curiosity about something like this would be totally inappropriate from a boy of fourteen. So, I tried to ignore my mother's question. But she insisted. She kept on pinching me, so many times that our silent dialogue attracted the eyes of the lawyer Ferial and she smiled. She thought my mother was longing to taste the pomegranate, and she held out half the fruit toward us. But my mother shook her head. And then she repeated the hand gestures she had made. The lawyer laughed. She put the fruit on her blanket, which was spread over the floor of the trailer, raised her palms, and opened them in our direction and bent the thumb of her right hand.

'She's in her ninth month', I whispered to my mother. But the pregnant lawyer's sign was so clear that my mother understood it without my words. My mother opened her hands and tipped her head back to look up. The clouds had begun to migrate, in closely packed convoys moving across the sky. Next, she rubbed her hand across her thin, pale face with a quick motion. This was a sign that she was praying for the lawyer, who sat down slowly and heavily and resumed picking out the seeds from the halved pomegranate and eating them with gusto.

The tractor made its way along a winding road between rocky outcroppings and then came out onto a straighter road where there was not so much traffic. My uncle pushed the tractor to go a little faster. It wasn't more than a quarter of an hour before we reached a point near Kimar where the road became very crowded. A long line of vehicles was inching along, and then it stopped. Suddenly, Ferial shrieked. The two old women hurried over to her. A couple of minutes later, they ordered me and Alan out of the trailer. Immediately. We were the only two males still in there.

I understood that this order had something to do with the belly of the pregnant lawyer, Miss Ferial. I climbed out and helped my brother down. My mother quickly and silently joined the pair of old women as they began their emergency work. When she saw us watching the scene with great curiosity she came over and shut the door of the trailer in our faces, smiling. Then she went back to the two old women and Ferial, whose screaming hadn't even paused.

'What's happening?' my uncle asked me. I told him about Ferial the pregnant lawyer, and how she had shrieked just as we were reaching this spot where everyone was stopped. My uncle's face went white, and he pressed his lips together.

'She's going to have a baby? Right here? That's all we need.'

'Does it make any sense?' I asked, innocently.

'Yes, it makes sense, stupid', he replied testily. 'It makes a lot of sense. People still couple up when the bombs are falling, you know. Human beings don't stop having married lives, not even for a single second. Don't you know that human beings are always having sex?'

'How do you know, Uncle?'

'From the numbers. The statistics, you Uncle's Donkey. They say there are three births every second in the world. That means, every second there are three embryos forming inside these dumb wombs. Not to mention all the sex that doesn't lead to pregnancy or the sex that ends in abortions, or ... or ... or ... and so on and so forth. This means fucking is an operation that never stops. Wars don't stop it and neither do natural disasters or anything else. Nothing is capable of stopping human beings from wanting to fuck.'

'Okay, so then what are we going to do when she has the baby?'

'We'll dance, you idiot! Ya Dubbat al-Khal! Your Uncle's Dancing Bear—what will we do, you ask? Of course, we won't do anything. Anything at all. We'll just keep on going toward Aleppo as if nothing has happened. Just like war and its catastrophes didn't keep this woman and her husband from having a baby, her baby won't keep us from continuing on our refugee way.'

The woman's screams were very, very intense by now. We could hear the two old women telling her to *push*, *push*! My brother Alan stared at me and began laughing. He was trying to cover up his embarrassment, I knew.

Suddenly my uncle shouted 'What's this?!' at me. He was staring at me. He looked baffled.

'What's what?' I asked him, fearfully. He was staring at me.

'Your neck. It's your neck, Kamo. It looks like the trunk of a very old tree. What's going on?'

I put my hand up to my neck. It did feel very rough. When I lowered my hand, I could see white marks on my fingertips.

'I'm afraid maybe I'm turning into a fish?' I said, laughing. My skin felt like fish scales, I thought. But my uncle was completely serious as he leaned in closer.

'I'm not joking, Kamo. Let me see. Omigod ... your skin is all dried out and cracked, and it is dead white. I'm worried that maybe you've got some kind of psoriasis. I'm not a doctor, but this doesn't look like anything normal. When we get to Aleppo we'll go see a specialist.'

A long, loud groan from Ferial cut off our conversation. My brother Alan jumped up and scurried over to sit under a tree where the shade would protect him. The sky was clear and the air was calm, but there was no end to the din made by all of these fleeing people who were huddled in the backs of pickups or crammed into tractor trailers, nor to mention the sound of all of these marching feet, belonging to the masses of evacuees filing along the sides of the road, their feet encased in mud left by the spring rain the day before. Every face out there was pale with fatigue, the exhaustion and the sense of being abandoned streaming down like tears, all the fear and terror, words on everyone's lips that no one could understand, not even the people whose mouths were forming them.

The only sounds I could hear that were clear and unmistakable were Ferial's shrieks and moans. A mother who was about to give birth to a child on the open road—in the middle of the road, in fact—in the trailer of a farm tractor, one amongst all of these now-homeless people fleeing the bombings.

One of the old women stood up on the side of the trailer nearest to us. 'Can someone bring some hot water?' she asked.

My uncle just laughed. I could barely hear his voice when he said, 'And while we're at it, don't you want us to find someone to marry you off to, as well?' Then he looked at me, and he spoke clearly now, his tone sarcastic. 'This raving woman thinks we're in a five-star hotel.'

It was at this moment that the family of Uncle Naaso descended from the trailer. Two boys, seven and eight years old. Their mother stayed in the trailer to help out the two old women and my mother as they tried to get Ferial's baby to come out.

'What's your name?' I asked the first boy.

'Hannan,' he answered, yawning.

'And you, what's your name?'

'Mannan.' He was rubbing his eyes.

'You were in their father's house for days and days, and you didn't even learn their names?' my uncle exclaimed. 'Little Donkey, you—Uncle's Little Donkey.'

'Hannan and Mannan', I said. 'The problem is the names, it isn't my memory, Little Donkey's Uncle!'

My uncle laughed when he heard me throwing the nickname back at him. He went on laughing, and then he strolled over to an olive tree and sat down beneath it and began playing something from a very famous song by the late artist Ali Tijo, called 'Yara Milisa'.

A whole band of youths and men quickly gathered round. They

listened to the sad music in total silence. I saw men whose faces were wrinkled by long lives wiping their tears on the edges of their red and black shimaghs. I watched as some of the men walked away. Maybe they wanted to leave before they could spill any more tears, which might threaten to flood out their eyes.

***

Uncle Naaso's wife stood up suddenly in the trailer of her husband's tractor and began ululating.

'What is it?' This was my uncle shouting, as he put down his bouzouki and walked toward her.

'The woman's had her baby, and everything is fine.'

'Alhamdulillah.' My uncle slung his bouzouki over his shoulder.

'But the poor thing has had a baby girl.'

'So what? The important thing is that the mother is safe and well.' My uncle climbed into the driver's seat. He put his instrument down next to it. Then he climbed out again.

'Don't you want to play something, uncle?'

'Ferial has played the sweetest melody. She's had a girl and there are no beings on earth sweeter than girls. True, I never married, but my mother always wished she had another girl, and she wished it so hard that we all wished it as much as she did.'

I thought about Maysoon, my sister sliced in two by an exploding barrel on her birthday, on one terrible day in eastern Aleppo. I bowed my head and began thinking about everything that had happened in this strange life of ours. My mother, the sad mute woman. Her parents' only child. My mother Layla, daughter of my grandmother Nazli who was snatched away by a missile shot by a warplane as she was getting treatment in a hospital in Aleppo.

We stayed in this spot for about an hour. I watched as the two old women climbed out of the trailer and buried something next to a tree trunk. Something that was wrapped up in a rag. I was aching to know what it was.

'That's women's business,' my uncle said. 'Stay away, Kamo. Maybe it's the afterbirth she buried.'

'Afterbirth?

'Yes, afterbirth.'

'Only a mad person would bury an *after birth*. That's what we're looking for. That's what we need for this long suffering of ours, Uncle.'

'The *afterbirth*, Your Uncle's Donkey, is what's left of the placenta. Something a little like a disc that falls out with the baby. It has no use after the birth. It has to be buried quickly so that cats or other animals don't try to get it.'

'Well, what would happen, I mean, if a really clever cat did get hold of it?'

'The baby would be as curious as you are, Donkey.'

We walked over to the trailer. We began listening to the talk of the women gathered around Ferial: the two elderly women and Uncle

Naaso's wife. We could hear everything they said.

'Name her Kimar, because she was born here, near this village.'

'No, name her Jullanar. After the last fruit you took, a fine pomegranate from Basuta.'

'Why not name her Afrin? Afrin is the name that's most suited to her. Afrin witnessed, is still witnessing, a painful trial like the trial this poor girl and her mother are witnessing.'

I don't know exactly what name my mother, who wouldn't speak, suggested. In fact, I don't know how she would have suggested it. But like everyone else, I heard Ferial's weak voice as she rejected all these suggestions and then said, in a tone of voice that meant this was it, 'I will name her Qafila. Caravan. Yes, that's right, Qafila. And I hope that our Qafila reaches a safe haven.'

***

I had begun to learn that every vehicle, every farm tractor trailer, and indeed every single person in this sad caravan, in this fleet of cars and file of people that continued as far as the eye could see, had griefs to bear that were heavier than mine.

'When everyone's being plundered, it might as well be a wedding.'

During the time we spent in Aleppo, my Gramma Nazli always said this proverb of ours when she was trying to lighten my mother's pains and remind her that there were thousands of people like my father who had gone missing.

It was certainly true, what my grandmother said. Heavy pain, when it is shared among thousands of human beings, feels a little lighter. The sharpness of it softens. One single person can't possibly bear the weight of a whole big disaster, like the Afrin catastrophe. But when it is spread among thousands of people, it gets a little easier. It changes into a lot of individual pains suffered by individual people, and mostly they can handle that much. But if the pain goes on being the lot of only a few people, then not all the chalks in the world, plus all the pens in the world (and there are too many of them to count) won't be enough to write down the extreme awfulness of it.

My uncle was leaning his trunk against the trunk of that old olive tree and looking at his mobile phone. I went over and sat down next to him, looking at the small screen along with him. One of the channels was airing a detailed report on the looting that armed groups were carrying out in the villages and towns of Afrin after they'd attacked the district and occupied it. In one segment, which went on for only about half a minute, I saw my green bike held tightly by a fighter from the Hamzaat Brigade that was attached to the Free Syrian Army. He was wearing camouflage and his face was covered by a black beard. He was staring straight into the camera and smiling as he gripped the handlebars. Then he raised two fingers of his right hand in a victory sign and shouted, 'Booty! Booty from the infidel Kurds! Praise be to God who gave us victory over them!'

'Victory over whom, you whore's son!' shouted my uncle, his eyes bulging. 'Over whom?'

I felt like I was paralyzed. And then I shouted, 'They've stolen my bike!'

'Khadraa?'

'Yes! They stole it. And there it is. I know it like I know the palm of my own hand.' I jabbed my finger at the green bike before my uncle paused the video.

'It's ours, victory!' the man gripping the handlebars of my bike repeated. It was the same man I'd seen in my sleep, the one who slapped me so hard he made me scared enough to pee. He shouted, announcing his victory, and the others began to chant, singing and dancing and celebrating their victory. They had been looting the shops, stealing jerry cans of oil, computers, fridges, washing machines, blankets, clothing, motorbikes, cars, and tractors. Everything. They plundered all of Afrin.

My uncle was repeating his words, grinding his teeth. 'Who did you get this victory over, you pimp? Who?'

'It's a victory for all the Syrians, Uncle. Some of them got victory over others.'

Trying to keep back a tear, my uncle answered me. 'Yes, Kamo. It's true, what you're saying. Victory for all the Syrians. And defeat for all the Syrians, too, nephew. There's not a winning party that didn't get defeated. There's no armed group that wasn't defeated. There's no community that's gotten victory. This is a puzzle that fighters in our country have never understood, and they still don't get it. The one who has secured a victory has filled the world with gravesites and with people who have terrible afflictions and wounds, widows and widowers and orphans, and with the missing and the gaoled. And the ones who've been defeated are just the same. So what difference is there between victory and defeat in these wars, if the result is the same, for the winners as much as the losers?'

I nodded, thinking about Khadraa, my green bike, and how it had managed to get to Sharraan—all the way to Afrin District! Was it really my bicycle or did it just look like my bicycle?

No, it was my bicycle. I knew it was. From the bell on the right handlebar, from the silky red streamers dangling from the handgrips, from a lot of other things—I knew it was mine. My green bike. My Khadraa.

So that means they looted my uncles' home. They stole our most loved things. And all our belongings—our blankets, fridge, clothes, everything we left behind.

'It's my bike. They stole it, Uncle.'

'The one who steals a revolution steals everything.' My uncle's voice was very harsh and angry.

'Are revolutions bicycles, meaning robbers would steal them?' I asked him.

My uncle didn't say anything.

***

I was very upset at the sight of the armed man in the video, hugging my green bicycle to his chest. The same man I saw in my dream. It was beyond belief. How this could happen I didn't know. But I did know perfectly well that this man in the camouflage uniform with the black beard—I mean the thief who was smiling into the camera as he held on to the handlebars of my bicycle—was happy because he was probably going to take it to his son who was waiting for him in some town in Syria. Maybe to Izaz, Sharraan's neighbouring town. Or to Aleppo. Or maybe he was one of our neighbours back in Manbij! Maybe his son was even an evacuee like me, from Ghouta for instance, who was living in one of the houses that the mercenaries settled into in Afrin and other places. Or he was living in a tent in some camp for internal refugees in Idlib. Karama Camp, for instance, run by UNICEF. Yeah, 'Honour Camp'. These names of our camps—how they make people laugh! Mukhayyim al-Karama, Mukhayyim al-Muqawama, Mukhayyim al-Battikh al-mubasmar. Generosity Camp, Camp of the Resistance, Camp of Watermelon Too Rotten to Eat!

It's true, I don't know where the town of that fighter who stole my bike is located, but I am very sure that his son is expecting his father to come back from war all in one piece, just like I'm expecting my bike to be returned to me, and my father, Surgeon Dr Farhad, to be returned to me.

It struck me suddenly that Uncle Naaso's wife hadn't asked about her husband.

'Didn't this woman notice that her husband isn't here?' I asked Uncle Ali.

'No. But it isn't something she's too concerned about, anyway. This is just the usual business in wartime. You wake up and you see that someone is gone. You don't need to ask.'

Just then, I heard the wife of Uncle Naaso calling out to Uncle Ali. 'Where did Naaso go, Ali?'

My uncle answered immediately. 'He went to Afrin, said it was important business. He'll be back soon.'

Then my uncle got to his feet, to resume driving the tractor. I got up with him, my heart in pieces over my bicycle. On my face, Ali could read the grief the scene of that theft had left in me. 'Don't be sad, Kamo,' he tried to console me. 'The important thing is that we've hung onto our souls. We're still breathing. If we'd stayed there, those people would have stolen our souls, too.'

I didn't say anything. I walked beside him feeling very sad. We heard a lot of people talking about the widespread plunder all across Afrin. Like me, a lot of folks had recognized their stolen belongings when they saw the videos. They were defeated, subdued. *La hawla lahum wa-la-quwwata*. No power, no strength ... among humans. They turned their backs on Afrin as it was being raped. There was pain beyond description in their hearts.

After we left the village of Kimar behind, I saw hundreds of evacuees passing by on foot, on both sides of the road. Old men. Elderly women holding little children by the hand. Or maybe it was the children who were holding the old women by the hand. They were all sinking into the disgusting mud left by the rains, and their heads were bent as low as the ground. They didn't raise their heads even when the goddamned Turkish planes went back to making a huge racket in the skies high above them. There's no doubt that this mass of silent evacuees were themselves owners of tractors and pickups and cars and motorbikes that the raiders of Afrin had stolen, those people who were so proud of looting all the belongings of people, as they appeared on TV screens and in photographers' lenses, that they didn't even think about showing the slightest embarrassment or shame.

'Do you know the man who slipped and lost his footing a few minutes ago and fell into the mud?' my uncle asked me. He was talking about a man we saw fall on his face in the mud. He had been walking alongside our tractor.

'I don't know anyone from Afrin.'

'This man owned two microbuses that ran the Afrin-Rajo and Afrin-Basuta routes. When we were in Uncle Naaso's house, I saw him once, in the garage. His mates were very worried about the fate of their vehicles, and he said: 'The two microbuses went to Rajo a week ago, and they haven't come back. The armed groups there must have confiscated them for their own use. Alhamdulillah I still have two feet I can walk on.' D'you know, Kamo, if those savages could, they would steal people's feet, too.'

Under a White Tent's Roof

Things didn't change much for us after the birth of little Qafila. We went on waiting for the caravan to move, shading ourselves beneath a big and very old olive tree. Finally, the opportunity came after two very anxious days of waiting. We lived through those days crammed into the tractor trailer near Kimar. Then we continued our migration by way of the safe corridor toward Aleppo. Word spread that al-Ziyara Crossing leading into Aleppo had opened, and so the long, long convoy that had been at a complete standstill finally began moving in the direction of the crossing. It had been bombed by Turkish planes about a month before, to prevent Syrian regime reinforcements from arriving to help the fighters in Afrin.

I was very frightened when I learned, from what people were saying, that we were heading for al-Ziyara Crossing. I was afraid that the bombing might begin again, since we had heard terrifying stories told by women and children about the massacres that had gone along with the bombings by Turkish war planes.

The road leaving Kimar was very rough. It was rocky, unlike the green route from Afrin as far as Ayn Dara. The further we got from Afrin, the worse it was: more suffering, more fear, more confusion. The road got more uneven and more difficult. It was full of rocks, and there were more checkpoints, and different ones, from one day to the next.

'You need a map to get around in this cursed geography. Barriers and checkpoints everywhere, and a person doesn't know who to follow. What's important is paying at every checkpoint so you can get through.' That's what my uncle said, and then he kicked the huge back tyre of the tractor. We were stopped between two checkpoints.

These were what scared people the most. For instance, there was the matter of young males who hadn't gone into military service and were demanded by one group or another. The people in charge at a particular checkpoint didn't know when to stop them and take them in and lock them up. There was a lot of deliberate humiliation, insults everywhere. There was the likelihood of being stopped to wait for hours. Hunger, thirst, a yearning to pee and poop, which refugees held in until they could find the right time and place.

The fear kept us company until we reached a place where some comrades from the Party were there to receive us. They told us it was impossible to go on to Aleppo. The regime had blocked all the routes and they weren't allowing anyone, no matter who it was, to continue on, to reach Aleppo. And there were more checkpoints there, where they were arresting and locking up anyone who was the right age for military service. We were more worried than ever.

'Dammit! Isn't there any end to this tunnel? We're exhausted!' my uncle shouted.

'Never mind, comrades, never mind. We'll take you to the Resistance's camp.' That was what a fighter in his forties, one of the comrades, called out. He had thick moustaches that looked like the handlebars on my bicycle which had been stolen by the men of the Hamzaat Brigade.

When we entered the camp, we had to leave the tractor behind. We all climbed out. Me, my mother, Alan, Uncle Naaso's family, the two old women, and Lawyer Ferial and her baby. Now we had become official refugees, in this camp located north of the village of

Fafin, which later on they began to call Barkhudan, which meant 'the resistance'.

***

In that weird place, the camp belonging to the Resistance, people were more confused than ever about this situation they found themselves in. People looked like they had just risen from their graves and the angels had driven them to the assembly point for the Day of Resurrection. Tens of thousands of people had fled from Afrin and its surrounding villages and environs, fearing the violence of the Turkish Army and the mercenaries who worked with them. Those troops didn't show mercy to anyone. Strafing from guns and airplanes were coming from one direction, while from the other came attacks by the mercenary units who were supported by the Turkish forces. They were attacking and looting the emptied-out villages and towns. The whole area around Afrin was transformed into a hell that not even jinnis and devils could abide.

But none of this was so strange. What was strange was the goings-on in that camp full of white shit. I mean, the white tents with the blue fronts. Through the microphones, we heard one harangue after another about how anyone who wanted to return to Afrin was a traitor.

Traitor! The one who wants to go and live in the shadow of Erdoğan. Traitor! The one who wants to spend his life in the shadow of the flag of the Turkish Army of Occupation. Traitor ... traitor ... traitor ... We will not return until it is a Liberated Afrin. We will not return until we can return with our heads held high. We promise you this. Staying, and staying resolute, staying firm, in the camps is one kind of resistance. We will resist and oppose the Wolf of Anatolia and his hyena followers with our steadfastness and through enduring the hardships of life here. Living in a tent is better than living in the shadow made by the occupier's flag. Honour comes before everything!

Personally, I didn't understand the point of any of this. Anyway, I had not really taken in what had happened to me and my little family throughout this whole time, the time since I reached an age when I began to understand things. I mean, ever since the Free Syrian Army troops in Manbij were crushed in 2014 and Daesh, along with its black flags, paraded into the city streets and alleys.

When the microphones kept repeating these words of theirs, my uncle said, 'Those people are confused and they want to confuse us along with them.'

Hmm. My uncle also didn't have a convincing explanation for the extreme chaos and clashing contradictions that I saw around me. At one point, the comrades would be ordering people to leave their villages and prepare to evacuate as internal refugees. Then, at a second moment, they would forbid people to leave. In fact, they intervened with some people who had already begun their journeys, trying to force them to change direction and go back to their native villages. But then, once we were in the camp, they began shouting over their microphones that anyone returning to Afrin would be considered a traitor supporting the Turkish occupation. *Fawda ghayr khallaqa* is what my uncle called it. A worthless, barren chaos.

'The regime's checkpoints are not allowing people to return to Afrin or to keep going toward Aleppo. Same with the comrades' checkpoints. The thieves' checkpoints, of course, block anyone who might by chance even think about returning home. How did all these people come to an agreement about leaving the people from Afrin to live out in the open while they watched their city being plundered and stripped, and their land violated? Everything comes down on us, ya Allah! Even you up there, too?" This was what an old woman from the village of Barimjah who was sitting at the doorway of her tent exclaimed as she waved her cane at the distant sky.

A man of about her age walked over toward her. He sat down beside her and said hello. 'They've totally confused us,' he said. 'And they're still doing it. In the beginning, they encouraged people to get out. Then they went back on that and made everyone stay in Afrin, which was packed with people who had evacuated their towns and villages. And now they're preventing people from returning, and they're calling it *being a traitor*.'

'Yes, that's true. Those folks don't know what they're doing. It's a huge disaster. And they didn't see it coming.' The old woman was shading her eyes from the sun as she spoke. I was standing close enough to the two old people that I could easily listen to their talk. A few minutes later, they were joined by a man with only one foot who was hobbling along on crutches. He said hello and sat down, extending his sound leg and cursing his crutches.

'If only I had two good feet. W'Allahi, I left Afrin only to become a martyr.'

'A lot of people had good jobs, and they had feet, too, but when the airplanes began circling over our heads they grew some extra feet and fled before anyone else did, so don't think too much of yourself,' snapped the old woman, and I could hear laughter. I left the three of them with their cackles and walked until I had passed two more tents. Near the third one, a man wrapped up in a blanket caught my attention. He was leaning against the door into his tent, his eyes closed against the bright sunlight. He was talking. I stopped and began to listen. I thought he was talking to himself. Here in the camp, I'd often seen men and women talking to themselves, and I had seen it when we were on our refugee journey, too. I was standing not far away from him, and I began really trying to listen hard and to make out what he was saying.

'They wanted to make us into human shields and protect themselves with us, instead of protecting us.'

He paused, and then he went on talking. 'Don't you remember, Nisrin, when the grip loosened and people emigrated in the thousands and we were with them?'

So, now I knew he was talking to a woman, probably his wife. She must be inside the tent.

'How could you not remember, ya Dujaja! It's only been two weeks since it happened.'

Inside the tent, I heard a noise I couldn't quite identify. It must be his wife answering him. It sounded like she was making it clear that she was very irritated at being called a stupid hen. The man, his eyes still closed, persisted.

'Yes, yes, you *are* a stupid hen. Dujaja, that's what you are! You don't remember anything that doesn't please you. You remember the dress your neighbour had on at the wedding five years ago. You remember the set of teacups that So-and-so gave to So-and-so when she moved to a new house, ten years back. And then you don't remember something that happened two weeks ago. Anyway, when we were a few kilometres from Afrin, we were challenged by some armed men linked to the Party. They'd started piling up stones to block the escape route. The mouths of their guns were pointed at us. Weren't you one of the women, after all, who marched right toward them and tore down the wall of rocks they'd made, so that our caravan could start moving again?'

At this point, a woman's voice rose from inside the tent. 'I remember, I remember.' She grumbled. 'And it was more than a few armed boys standing and confronting that flood.'

I left them arguing and went on, passing the tent of a poor woman who had been burned one day after reaching the camp. She had wanted to cook something for her children, on the fire, after the exhaustion and hardship of three days out in the open without any hot food. But the tent caught fire and all their possessions burned. She was burned so badly that the injuries left her unable to move, and she didn't get proper medical treatment. The ruins of the burnt tent were still there; no one had bothered to remove them. I went by fast, heading toward the next tent.

A lot of these tents, which had been put up in such a hurry, were silent. I mean, whoever was supposed to be in them was silent. I went by those tents as if I were passing by a row of graves. Other tents, though, were full of sound and movement. Children playing and shouting at each other, women talking among themselves, men holding conversations in loud voices. I heard a lot of things said, and many terrifying stories about evacuation and its terrors. I thanked God that we had had Uncle Naaso's tractor, which made things easier for us. We hadn't had to deal with the kind of extreme fatigue these people had felt, walking on foot for three days from Afrin to this camp, sleeping out in the open with nothing over their heads, in the fields or next to boulders or maybe in a cave.

***

As I went deeper and deeper inside the camp that day, I noticed a group of men in front of the doorway of one tent, a bit further on from where I stood. They were sitting on plastic chairs, their tired faces raised to catch the sun, the clouds their cigarette smoke made hanging over them like a thick fog. By now, I was tired of wandering around and finding my way through all these tents, and I was thinking how much I needed a little break. I went over to that group of men, propelled by my curiosity about what they were saying. I sat down on the ground not far away and began listening so hard that I could hear the sound of their breathing and the noise their lips made as they blew white smoke high into the wide emptiness.

They were all telling their tales of leaving home, of being evacuees. The stories all began in the same way—or rather, it was one story that was repeated as many times as there were men to tell it. But one of them looked sadder than the rest. Telling his story was clearly painful for him. It was nothing like our stories. Everyone here had their own narratives, but in the end, they were all about how they had left Afrin and the surrounding villages. Except his. He told the story of his attempt to return to Afrin.

'When it all started, I decided I would go ahead and leave, and get to Aleppo where I could join my sons who live in al-Ashrafiyya. We were received very well by the people of the Shi'i town of Nubbul. They really gave us a good welcome. But there were a lot of us. The mosques and the schools there didn't have enough room to hold us all. Some people began spreading out their mats on the pavements and roadsides. And some weak souls began renting out the paved spaces in front of their homes to people seeking refuge for an outrageous amount of money. Even trying to find a place to relieve yourself, folks—even that came with a price. W'Allahi l-'azim! In fact, there was one price for someone who wanted to relieve himself and another for a person who needed to sit. Not to mention the business of food and drink.

'Anyway ... so, then I heard that you could find the people smugglers if you went to the cafes, and that they were making big deals with anyone who wanted to leave home and flee to Aleppo. The prices went up and up, and I didn't have any money with me, anyway. I don't even know in the first place how I left my home, fleeing when they began targeting the neighbourhood. I was like a madman, just running through the alleys, round and round. Until I found myself crammed into the back of a pickup heading from Basuta to Ayn Dara. The point, folks, is that I tried to borrow some money from people I knew, but no one would lend me anything. I went to one of the smugglers and I told him, "All of my children are in Aleppo, if you can try to take me there, after I get there they'll pay you what you ask for. My oldest is a doctor and the next one has a well-known pharmacy, and for certain they'll return the favour doubled."

'The smuggler just laughed at what I'd said. "Ya Hajji," he said, "no one buys fish when they're still swimming in the sea. If you want to get to Aleppo, pay up first. And we have to bribe them at the checkpoints. No one gets through those without paying, even if it's Imam Husayn himself. I can lower the price for you a little. The other guys take 600 dollars a person. Just give me 500 and I'll take you to al-Ashrafiyya."

'Just listen to this idiot! He thought I could produce dollars as if I were a hen laying eggs. He didn't know that I can't even empty my bowels because of the constipation I've been suffering, from all the horrors and exhaustion of this flight.'

At this, I nearly burst out laughing, but I suppressed my giggles. Still, I could hear the men guffawing at what the man had said. He laughed, too. He lit a new roll-up from the one that was nearly gone and went on.

'Anyway, brothers, all my attempts ended in failure. No one lent me anything, not even half a lira. And anyway, the smugglers—whoever and wherever they are—they worship money. They call the qirsh *papa* and the lira *mama*. What could I do? Stay in Nubbul? Impossible. It was already costing too much. The more migrants in town, the higher the price to stay in any sort of lodging or shelter, and the more it cost to be smuggled out. I thought about returning home. I said to myself, "I'll go back even if I have to do it on my own two feet. I'll crawl if I have to, in order to get to my own home where I was the sultan. I'll even go the whole way on my knees, if it means going back to my beautiful Afrin."'

The man stopped talking abruptly. In the half-light, I could see tears glistening in his eyes. In all my life, I hadn't known men who cried. I felt so sad for him, and I was engulfed by an overwhelming feeling of anger and despair. I wanted to get up, but what kept me tethered there was that I wanted badly to hear the rest of his story. I put my head between my hands like my mother was always doing, and I listened closely to the rest of what he had to say.

'Does it make any sense for Afrin to become a second Palestine? For us to cry over our fields of olive trees just like the Palestinians wept over their orange and lemon orchards, and how they're still mourning them to this day? They say the armed men from the Ghouta are going to settle in our homes and our fields, and that they'll take their families with them. They say that green buses have been leaving towns in the Ghouta heading for Afrin and Jarablous.

I don't know, but I heard on the news that the armed groups will leave Duma and Arbin and other towns in the Ghouta which the Russians have bought up to serve the interests of the regime. That's in exchange for Afrin, which Turkey bought up to serve the interests of those fighters. A bazaar, wAllahi—it's a bazaar like no one's ever seen, even in the cafes of Nubbul with their haggling over the price of people smuggling. Hey, people—hey, world—are we the folks who went to destroy the Ghouta and bring famine on its people? Is this what justice is? Is this what God decreed in all His books? How can they go and live in my house when, here in this tent, my belly is so hungry I'm in pain? How can they not allow me to get to my sons in Aleppo, leaving me a prisoner in this miserable vile camp? My field is gone and for sure my oil press has been stolen, and my home has become the property of strangers. Do you accept this, God?'

The man raised his head and his hands to the sky, which was rapidly filling with clouds.

'Even returning to Afrin is only a dream now,' he went on. You could tell from his dejected voice how completely his spirit had been broken. 'Imagine—I took the route by the village of Sawghanka. It was the last remaining bit of safe corridor. First, I was stopped at a regime checkpoint where they asked me for more money than the smugglers in Nubbul were demanding. See—returning to Afrin would cost me more than evacuating to Aleppo! Of course, I didn't go on. I heard later that even if you get by the regime checkpoint without too much damage, the checkpoint of the Islamist battalions taking orders from the Turkish Army will demand even more, a lot more, and even if these battalions are in the checkpoints of Kimar and Turindah, they're not satisfied with having just your money. They order you to leave all your possessions, everything you own, and then you have to go on to Afrin on foot.'

No sooner had the man uttered the word 'Afrin' than he let out a horrendous moan. It was really frightening. First, his body swayed to the right, then collapsed. The other men jumped up and went over to him and began shouting things I couldn't make out, except for the word *ambulance.*

I never knew who that man telling his sad story was. But that evening, I learned that he had died after being rushed to the medical unit. It was a blood clot, and it must have throttled him while he was talking.

***

That was the same day I lost my Safra, my little chalk. I couldn't find her again. I thought back to all the places I had been while I was wandering around the camp. I went back and looked everywhere—in any spot where I might possibly find my chalk. I searched every corner of that camp, but it was no good.

I missed her, my companion on this whole long journey as evacuees. I told her everything. I described people to her, and all the roads and byways; I told her about the splendid brilliant green olive tree groves we passed on the way from Afrin and all the way to Ayn Dara; I shared stuff that was sad and some happy thoughts, too. I brought her with me to the camp to be my companion, the one I told all my griefs and my joys, the disasters and terrors that happened to refugees as well as the delights of my adventures in the village of Sharraan. I wanted to tell her about how I saw a man die because he had been so beaten down by it all. I searched and searched for her, but I didn't find her anywhere. Where could she have disappeared to? I wanted so badly to tell her what had happened to us since arriving in this camp, and I wanted to write a line with her that was ringing in my ears like the electric bell we were forced to hear at school. I wanted to write on the outside of our tent: Fuck this Camp. In fact, if I'd found my chalk I would have written it at the entrance to the camp. Fuck this Camp!

I also wanted to tell her about this strange illness I was getting, the symptoms that were appearing on my skin. As soon as we landed on the territory occupied by this camp, I started to feel a terrible dryness in my skin. It was beginning to feel like rough wood. Or, it's better to say it was like chalk. Whenever I touched it, from my face to my neck to my stomach and thighs and butt and even down to my feet and toes, I found my fingertips covered with a chalklike powder. It was a very weird calcification that was spreading day by day. Even my penis was rough to the touch and had gone white.

When I complained about it to my uncle, he tried to comfort me. 'Maybe it's just some kind of condition that causes shrivelling.

'Shrivelling?' I asked, finding it impossible to believe.

'Yes, shrivelling. Or do you think you've been attacked by the evil eye, my precious gazelle?'

'Didn't you tell me, when we were still on our way here: "Your skin is dried out and it's cracking"?'

My uncle didn't answer, but he frowned as he looked at me. His expression was grumpy.

'Yes', I added. 'You said that, and you even promised to take me to a specialist in Aleppo.'

My uncle nodded. 'That's true, Kamo. I did promise you that. And now I promise you again: if we get out of this camp, I will take you to the very best dermatologist there is in the city of Aleppo.'

What about the camp doctor? He gave me aspirin and muttered some words we didn't understand. After we came back from the medical unit, my uncle began laughing as he toyed with the aspirin pack as if it were a book of matches.

'These doctors graduated from the Soviet Union, may it rest in peace. They are one-point-five degrees better than donkeys.'

'Maybe if he had given me a little box of chalk it would be better.'

'What would you do with that?'

'I'd write on the side of our tent: Fuck this Tent. And then I'd store the rest of the chalks for the griefs we haven't seen yet.'

My uncle laughed harder. And to the rhythm of his hard laughter, we went inside our white tent with the blue front which carried the logo of the United Nations High Commissioner for Refugees.

Zeytin Dalı: The Turkish 'Olive Branch'

And Noah waited another seven days, and again he sent out the dove from the ark; and the dove came back to him in the evening, and there in its beak was a freshly plucked olive leaf. So Noah knew that the waters had subsided from the earth. (Genesis 8. 1011).[1]

One morning, an unusual level of commotion just outside the tent woke me up. I opened one eye (it was my left eye), hoping this half-measure would not chase my sleep away. The door was partly open, and I peered outside. My mother was leaning against the left doorpost with her hands clasped behind her back. She was staring at some scene outside and there was a look of bewilderment on her face. Slowly, I realised that there must be something very worrying going on out there, and so I opened my right eye, too. I saw the Red Crescent van standing just outside our neighbour's tent—Ibrahim, whom we called Amm Iybo and who came from one of the villages of Maydanki. Even if I was lying on my mattress with my damned nappy full of piss, I could more or less see that something was going on just outside our tent—or rather, outside the tent across from us. The space between our tents was no more than a couple of metres. I felt too sluggish to get up, so I called out to my mother instead.

'What's going on out there? What are they doing?'

My mother's face was very pale and her expression hadn't changed. She jerked her right arm from behind her back and pointed to the facing tent, and then she waved her hand around in the air without

1 Based on the New Revised Standard Version.

saying anything. I didn't get it. Alan's head appeared inside the tent, poking far enough in that I could see half his body in the doorway.

'Kamo, Kamo! Its Hamida. They've taken her to the hospital.'

This wasn't really such a new piece of news. Every so often, Hamida would lose consciousness and fall to the ground. They took her to the doctor, or an ambulance came for her, and the medics worked on reviving her. Usually, it took only a few minutes. I hadn't ever paid much attention. Now, I tried to sit up, but I could feel my body going rigid. I slipped my hand between my thighs and felt how rough the skin was there, like the trunk of a gnarly old cypress tree. God! I couldn't believe it, really.

'I'm turning into a tree.'

That's what I said to myself, in a whisper, and then I burst out laughing as I imagined myself really becoming, say, an olive tree, a skinny young sapling maybe, perching in one of the fields around here. The Red Crescent van moved away, its irritating screech disappearing gradually amongst the tents. My mother lowered the blue cloth that covered the tent opening and she and Alan came back inside the tent. No one said a word. I stayed where I was, on my mattress, my body too stiff to move. I waited for a good moment to try to get up and deal with my usual morning shame.

My mother didn't say anything about it. She had gotten used to leaving me lying in bed. I'd been staying on my mattress in the mornings, just lying there, ever since I'd discovered I couldn't control my bladder through the night. She knew how embarrassing this was, so she left me alone. She'd gotten into the habit of making herself look busy with the needs of the household. I would wait until I saw the best possible opportunity to throw my abominable nappy into the rubbish, hoping to bury it out of sight, and then to deal with my bed and change the sheet. We had an unwritten agreement now, and we both stuck to it in a silent and comfortable collaboration.

But here was my brother Alan, showing a keen desire to talk. He sat down at my head, right next to the pillow, and said, as if he were reading me a story out loud, 'So Hamida has fallen again. I could see the foam, it was dribbling from her mouth. She began shivering really hard, and her eyes looked like huge white circles. Her mama was shaking her and crying and calling out to her to get up. Her grandfather, Uncle Iybo, came out and started rubbing her body, it was stretched out right there on the ground in front of their tent. But she just kept on shivering, and her body was shaking, harder and harder, and the white stuff kept coming out of her mouth. Kind of like shampoo bubbles. Then the ambulance came and took her away.'

'So, this isn't like all the other times?'

'Her mother said this was the first time the foam was coming out of her mouth like that. Kamo, why does white foam come out of anyone's mouth?'

I didn't have an answer and he got up and moved away from my mattress. I felt my body get a little more pliant and so I got myself up, but I was feeling heavy and slow. I took off the nappy while I was still under the bedcovers. I put it in a black plastic carrier bag. I dodged my brother and my mother and slipped outside. There was no rubbish bin here, so I went a bit further on, to the huge heap of rubbish in this part of the camp, and I threw my plastic bag into it. I tugged my pyjama bottoms down and peed near the dump, and then I came back. Near our tent, there was a big red water tank. I don't know why they picked such a painfully bright colour for the water tanks. I opened the tap and washed my hands and face and then headed back to our tent.

All the tents in this damned camp looked alike. Small children often got confused and went into the wrong one. A child would run in the door thinking it was their family's tent, and be startled to see the strange sad faces there. You could see the look of anxiety mixed with awkwardness on the child's face when they came out.

Just as I was reaching our tent the ambulance showed up again, stopping outside Amm Iybo's tent. I saw little Hamida getting out, clutching the olive branch which had never left her hand, it seemed, since the first day of our life in this wretched place. She looked unhappy as she stared into the rotten stinking air that surrounded all the tents.

***

When we first came to live here, I thought Hamida was just a slightly naughty kid whose head had been messed up by the war and so she had gone wild and a bit mad. She was about seven years old, and the olive branch never left her grip for even a moment. It wasn't anything more than a green branch about as long as three outstretched hands end to end. Several times, I watched as she tried to stick it in the ground. Then she would move about two metres away and start throwing rocks at it. She would be shouting. 'That one killed my father! The man's a criminal. The branch killed my father. Here's another rock for you, go to hell!'

Sometimes, we saw her around the tents using the branch to hit at a big rock or a length of metal or anything hard she came across. Or she would just slap it against the ground, yelling, 'I'll kill you like you killed my papa. I'll tear your limbs apart.'

Every so often, she fell into these short fits, but she always came to and then she began crying and hiding herself in her mother's hug. But this morning hadn't been the usual thing at all.

***

Was there anyone left who this whore of a war hadn't shitted on? Was there even one child left alive whose mind hadn't been destroyed by the terror of the awful things we went through? What had this little girl done to deserve that? They killed her father as she was watching. Where would this miserable child ever find safety or security?

One evening not long after we came to the camp, Amm Iybo flung a question at my Uncle Ali, but he didn't wait for a response. He just answered it himself. 'Ali, my son, believe me, there's nowhere safe left. It's not just Syria. The whole world—no where's safe, not anywhere.'

'Ayy wAllahi, Amm Ibrahim. Our family's the biggest example. We were in the eastern part of Aleppo. Then do you know what happened there—my mother died when one of the city hospitals was bombed. Then my little niece died in a barrel bombing in the neighbourhood of Masakin Hanano. My sister's husband had already been kidnapped by Daesh in Manbij. Our family was scattered—there's barely two of us together in one place. Me, for instance—I fled to Afrin looking for some peace and security. Then my sister and her sons followed me, after the terrible things that happened to them in Manbij and Aleppo. So here we are, prisoners held in the big fist of the unknown. We don't know what the future has waiting for us, not at all.'

I was listening to this depressing conversation between Amm Iybo and my uncle. The smoke from their cigarettes drifted up and covered their faces and blocked the sight of them from me. But the thick smoke didn't prevent me from hearing everything they said.

'We fled our village, Gamruk in the Maydanki area, coming to Afrin centre. The bombs were falling on the fields and the houses in that little village and there was nothing to do but get out of there. I swear by God, I swear, nephew, I am not the kind of man who runs away from home and abandons his fields. No. Amm Iybo doesn't leave his home no matter what happens, but life is precious and the responsibility for my family and their safety was on my shoulders. Those bombs, my son—they're blind. They can't see the difference between a civilian and a fighter. These people are just lying when they say they're being careful to spare the lives of civilians. They're such big liars! In fact, they're deliberately terrorizing any civilians who might still feel a little bit safe, just so they can be even more savage and strike whenever they please. The important thing is, Ali, to be able to flee from this cursed Olive Branch that was already whipping our backs and our chests, when we reached Afrin safely. We'd settled into my daughter's house in the Mahmudiyya area. But the damned Olive Branch didn't leave us alone there either. Those people began whipping our backs more viciously than before. What 'olive branch' is this, son? Some enormous Olive Branch bent on revenge and terror. What kind of olive branch is it when the only thing you can see on it is thorns up and down?'

Amm Iybo went silent and took a long draw on his cigarette. He yanked it out of his mouth and blew out a cloud of smoke as he tapped the ashes into a glass ashtray in front of him. He inhaled again, finishing the cigarette. In irritation, he stabbed the butt into the ashtray before going on.

'That black Friday—I'll never forget it as long as I live. Sixteenth of March. A few days before, the Turkish Army announced that they were opening a safe corridor from the south part of Afrin toward Turindah village. We wanted to grab this chance before the attacking troops could finish encircling the city. It was a cloudy day and there was a light rain coming down. The weather seemed like a good sign. This rain, I told myself, is telling us that the disaster we've been through is ending. Maybe we'll be able to hold on to a little bit of calm here in this city. At least, on really cloudy days, there aren't air raids. And we're civilians, we'll get away, we'll make good use of this safe corridor. That's what I was thinking.

'But only a few minutes later, the missiles were raining down on us. It was total hysteria. I shouted to my wife and all the family. We've got to get out now! is what I said.

'"Where?" my oldest son asked me. I told him I didn't know where. But my experience was telling me that this bombing was going to continue. The comrades had embedded themselves securely in the neighbourhood, fortressing themselves in. For the enemy to kill a fighter here, they would have to destroy an entire neighbourhood. That's the law of war. My granddaughter Hamida cried and gripped the hem of her mother's thobe and began screaming. "I'm afraid, Mama! They're going to kill us." I comforted her. I told her things, and I knew I was lying to her when I said them. "Don't be afraid. We'll be fine, we'll be safe. We're going to the *maljaa* now. We'll be there soon, at the refuge.' Aahh, Ali, aahh, my son, how many lies we adults tell the children when it's war. We lie to them about every last detail, because we believe that children don't understand anything. But children get what war means more than we do, Ali, my son. More than anyone, the children have the bitter taste of war on their tongues all the time.

'We left the house, my wife and I, my son and my daughter and her husband and the children. What we planned on doing was seeking safety in a nearby refuge, until the bombing would stop, and then we would leave Afrin. But only a few minutes after we left the house, even before we'd gotten out of al-Mahmudiyya, the missiles were coming down on us again.

"Mortars! Midfa" haawin!' That's what my son was shouting.

I told him, Hurry up, son. We don't have the time to figure out which bit is being bombed or with what! It's more important that we find some shelter in whatever safe space is closest. I hadn't even finished my sentence when I got a fragment in my thigh. And as soon as I sat down on the pavement to see how bad it was, I watched my son fall to the asphalt, in the middle of the street. He died immediately. He fell like a tree uprooted by a windstorm. And then, not far away, my daughter's husband fell, killed by another missile fragment. My middle child, my daughter, pregnant in her eighth month. She miscarried, after all of this. Umm Hamida was wounded on her hand. My other girl, too. The street filled up with dead bodies and severed limbs. I was shivering. I had very heavy pain, and I was calling out to my daughter to rescue me.'

Khala Farida, wife of Amm Iybo, had been silent during all these words of his, so silent that I thought she must be a mute. But suddenly, she interrupted her husband, objecting. 'You called your daughter? You're saying nonsense, Iybo. You're raving! Or maybe your wound made you lose your memory, too.'

'What, Farida? Didn't I call out to Sinem?'

'Sinem? You really are raving, old man. Sinem wasn't even with us.'

‘Then, who did I shout to, to rescue me?’

‘Me, you raving idiot. Me. And I came and I bound up your wound with a kerchief I always carry.’ Aunt Farida spoke with great confidence. She turned to my uncle and went on talking.

‘Son, wAllahi, I saw with my own eye tens of missiles coming down on the neighbourhood, even before one fell on us, when we were out in the street getting ready to leave. I don’t remember how many victims there were, exactly, but the street truly was full of corpses and blood was running as if it was a whole stream right there in the middle of the street. My little orphan granddaughter Hamida lost her mind when she saw her father drowning in his own blood. She began running here and there, in every direction, screaming. I left my son and my son-in-law, submerged in their blood, and ran after that poor little girl until I could grab her.’

The Mute

She's my mother.

This woman, whom this shit war has crushed and pounded into fragments, turning her into only half of what a human being is. This noisy war that's caused so much talk talk talk has frozen her tongue and swallowed her sweet words. The women in this camp just call her the Mute.

The Mute—my mother, Layla Aghazadeh, who graduated from the University of Aleppo, Faculty of Arts and Literature, Department of Arabic Literature. She graduated with distinction. The Mute—my mother who knew how to speak and write four languages. My mother—Layla, who silenced everyone else with her powerful logic whenever she started to speak. Daughter of Nazli, who was the daughter of Abd al-Hannan Aghazadeh from the village of Sharraan in Afrin province, this woman whose words flowed like honey from her mouth. But now she is more silent than a grave.

It wasn't the loud screech of airplanes or the noise of missiles or the scenes of death in Manbij that amputated my mother's tongue. It wasn't the jarring voices from the Daesh ranks ordering her to empty out the house in Manbij. It wasn't even the fact that leaving Manbij meant she was forced to leave the home she had furnished lovingly according to her taste. It wasn't having to live in my grandfather's house in Masakin Hanano in Aleppo as an internal refugee who had no say any more about anything and no resources at all.

What muted her was a fragment from a barrel bomb exploding on my little Sister Maysoon's birthday. A fragment probably no longer than a piece of chalk, which tore through my five-year-old sister's body and split it in two.

The Mute. Lalé—that's what we say in Kurdish.

But my mother was not really *lalé*, not physically. Not at all, never in her life. She knew several languages very well and she used to tell us stories, on some of those nights we lived through in Manbij and Aleppo. Lots of stories. More stories than the number of checkpoints and barriers we had to pass through in our journey as evacuees.

My mother—she's a university type, folks. That's who she is. She speaks well, even elegantly. But this incessantly noisy war muted her with the language of fire. With the language of despicable metal, the war silenced my mother. With the language of barrels exploding amongst the homes of Masakin Hanano, our neighbourhood where we sought shelter in Aleppo. And then my mother Layla got nicknamed The Mute.

***

In our silly camp, nothing upset me as much as people giving my mother the name Lal*é*: The Mute. They didn't call her The Professor. No—no one ever called her Ustaza Layla or even Umm Kamiran since she was my mother and I was the oldest kid. All the women there had names—family names, personal names—except my mother. She was *lalé*, The Mute.

I could remember very clearly how in Manbij, my mother Layla was a woman whose dignity people respected. First, because she was the wife of the surgeon, Dr Farhad, who headed Ibn Sina Hospital.

And then, because she was Ustaza Layla Aghazadeh, Instructor in Arabic. Even Daesh, with all their brutal arrogance, gave her a lot of slack because they didn't dare do otherwise. Daesh's cadres tried to get us to leave our home—they tried often—but they couldn't force it when faced with my mother's determination—her strong attachment to her home. She fortified herself there, protecting herself with my father's scent and memory. Nothing could get her out of that house except my grandfather who took her—unwilling as she was—to Aleppo.

But in that miserable camp, she had the name of The Mute. No one even asked her, 'Who are you? Where have you come from?'

'The Mute's Tent.' That's what the other people called our tent, even though there were three of us living here who could speak perfectly well, and in more than one language, too. Never mind. We were The Mute's children and the tent we lived in was The Mute's Tent. We were forced to accept this description until the damned war in our lands came to an end, this war which had been clattering on for six years now without anyone being able to silence it. We accepted that name for our mother and we accepted that we were more or less orphans until our lost father returned to us.

***

When I saw a morning smile on my mother's face, I knew she had seen my father in a dream. I would go up and ask her, sometimes by using gestures myself, if she had seen my father in her sleep. She would smile and nod.

Aaah. How much I longed for our mother to recount one of her dreams to us. Even if it was only half a dream. A little piece of dream.

I knew she saw my father in her dreams just as we saw him, too. So, I hoped that she would tell us even a sliver of one of her dreams. But she couldn't actually tell us what she had dreamed. What was odd about all of this was that she didn't try, not even once, to write out what she was feeling. Many times, I brought her a piece of paper and a pen, and I said, begging her, 'Mama, write something down. Even just one sentence. We want to know what has happened to you and why you aren't speaking.' I begged her many times, but nothing ever came of it.

She was mute, for sure. And being mute is death's twin sister. How painful, for me to live with my mother for four years without hearing her voice even once. Never hearing her scold, the way she used to scold me and my brother, her voice irritated and affectionate all at the same time. I even longed to hear her insults—those cutting words that were so gentle, even sweet. We missed her. We missed her smile, her laughter, and most of all, her fine bedtime stories that we liked so much. We thought longingly of her gentle silences, from the time just before she went mute. We missed seeing her put her small face between her hands and then gaze at us quietly and joyfully, then finally give us a smile. What have you done to us, War?

***

A few days before, my mother had been intent on making futuur pancakes. The weather was nice—it was a fine spring day.

'I want futuur like we always had in Sharraan', my idiot brother said.

‘A refugee, and you’re after the tastiest futuur? So—a beggar who sets conditions?’ I said to Alan. My mother gave me an angry look. Then she pointed to the eggs and made a circular motion with her hands as though she were beating something in a frying pan. Alan understood and nodded, giving us a naughty smile.

***

My mother lit the small camp stove and put the pan on it. She poured in some olive oil and sat down to whip the eggs in a small bowl. In and around Afrin, people cook everything in olive oil, from eggs to veal. Forget about vegetable oils or samna.

I was still lying in bed. I watched my mother as she whirled the eggs around with a metal spoon and sprinkled some salt and mint in, and a little red pepper, as usual. My nappy was soaked with my damned pee. I was waiting for the next possible opportunity to yank it off and stuff it into a plastic bag I had shoved under my pillow with this aim. Alan, though, was standing next to the pan like a starving cat about to pounce on a mouse. I heard him ask my mother if he could fry the eggs himself. My mother pushed him away, meaning ‘no’, but he wouldn’t accept it. He stamped his feet like a little kid. My mother had to give in to his demand and she passed him the bowl full of beaten egg.

Alan took the bowl with his left hand. He meant to pour the liquid into the pan. When he tried to firm his grip on the frying-pan handle with his left hand—the bowl was now in his right hand—he got flustered. He poured the egg into the pan and then I saw him lean over to put the bowl on the ground. In that exact moment, that is, as he bent down, he jerked the handle towards the side of his body, and the hot oil and frying egg tipped onto his hand and chest.

In less than a second, my head was ringing with clashing images. I had to make a crucial decision one way or the other, and then act on it and move on to the next step. Should I get out of bed and try to save my brother, with the possibility that my secret would be revealed—the humiliating fact that I peed in bed? Or grab what was an opportunity to pull off this stinking nappy and get rid of it outside and then try to save him?

My mother didn't know what to do. She didn't scream or shout, which surprised and upset me. How could she not yell or scream, trying to get someone to come and help when boiling oil was scorching her son? Then I remembered: of course not, since she was a mute. She didn't have a voice. She was like a thing, an object, not a being who lived and breathed. She was just like my lost, pale chalk. But even my chalk had a voice. A voice, on the blackboard, when the teacher wrote out lessons using it. So, then, this meant I was in charge, I was responsible for what would happen here, especially since my Uncle Ali the musician had picked up his instrument and gone off with it to join some of his friends, and he would spend the whole evening with them, late into the night.

I felt too dull and lifeless to get up. My skin was very dry, from my head all the way to my toes. I felt like I was floating freely inside the cavity of an oyster shell. I wasn't in any pain, but I just didn't have the energy to get out of bed.

Alan was screaming as I was probing my body with my dried-out fingers. His screams were so loud and so agonized that they seemed to rip open the tent and almost send it flying into the air. Finally, I decided I had to try to rescue him no matter what. I got out of bed calmly, gazing steadily at my mother's face which was rigid with terror. First, I extinguished the flame on the stove. Then I picked up my brother and pulled him away from the cursed stove and poured cold water all over him.

My mother was in a state of complete confusion. She began scurrying over to the door of the tent and, once there, she raised her hands in the direction of the clouded-over sky and implored God for help. Then she came back inside and stared at Alan, whose screaming didn't stop. In a moment she would be rushing from place to place inside the tent as though she were searching for something, after which she would go over and stare at Alan, who was yelling because of the intense pain, her eyes saying everything.

***

I got my brother Alan to the medical unit. The fat nurse, who was wearing the red vest of the Red Crescent, pulled off all my brother's clothes and examined his body, which had been seared by the goddamn oil. There were burns on both of his hands, across his chest, and on parts of his face. The fat nurse rubbed an ointment into the burns, made dressings and wrapped his arms in medical gauze. Finally, she gave us some painkillers for him.

'These are second-degree burns.' Her voice was cold and clinical. 'There isn't any great danger.'

I laughed to myself at this. 'Second degree? Are my brother's burns taking an exam, and this fatty nurse gets to mark them—first or second degree?'

As we were going back to our tent from the medical unit, I said to my brother—burned from the hot oil and held in my mother's tired embrace—'Never mind, second degree burns. It's not something to worry much about.' Then I tried to make a joke. 'You'll get a 'perfect', and first degree, next time you're burned, in sha allah.' My mother smiled. But Alan didn't smile, or laugh. In fact, he didn't show any reaction at all. Which hadn't been the case whenever I had teased him before.

***

Before we reached our tent, we came upon a group of people dancing a dabke. We learned later that a Party bigwig was visiting the camp.

Inside our tent, I laid my brother down on his mattress and then I went out, driven by curiosity to see what this Party official with his big moustaches and his paralysed hand would say to the crowds that these miserable tents had vomited out. Just at this moment, Uncle Ali showed up. I could see the fear plainly on his face.

'Where's Alan?'

'In the tent. Mother is taking care of him. He got burned. Hot oil.'

'What are you doing, leaving the tent? Why aren't you with your mother? She might need you for something.' My uncle didn't wait for my response. He walked toward our tent. I could see that he was very tense. He disappeared into its dark doorway, propelled by anxiety for his sister's little son.

The guy from the Party had assured himself by now that enough of a crowd had gathered to make it worth delivering his speech. He began looking at the exhausted, drawn faces of the people in front of him and he coughed, giving himself time to collect some thoughts. No sooner had the spray from his coughing spurted out than a horrible odour arose, and a gust of air helped to spread it across the camp. The smell made me dizzy, and I went back inside the tent without hearing the speech.

Outside, we could hear people's voices chanting grand slogans and applauding. They were sending threats and warnings to the Turkish Army. My uncle was gently holding my brother's hand. 'The biggest calamity is when you don't have any idea just how gigantic your calamity is,' he said, his voice as despairing as it could be.

Night of the Final Changes

As the patch of ground occupied by people coming to receive the senior Party official widened, their shattered voice boxes repeating the slogans calling for revenge against the Turkish occupiers and a return to Afrin, the patches of skin on my body that were turning into calcium widened, too. It began with my feet and crept up to my calves and then to my knees and thighs and butt. Although, on this particular overcast day, the calcification of my body was proceeding very gradually, I could definitely feel it. I was observing it moment by moment. I could tell how it was spreading slowly, the way the white cloud in a glass of araq expands and spreads when water is poured into the glass. My skin was growing white and dry. There wasn't any pain. In fact, what went along with this transformation was a feeling of overwhelming pleasure that is impossible to describe or compare with anything—except the pleasure I was given by the Widow Mazyat in the days when we were living in the town of Sharraan. I didn't tell anyone about what was happening to me. I knew it wouldn't be believed, and that I was about to experience a terrible ordeal, and I didn't know what the end of it would be. I kept this thought buried, the way I had hidden the business of my night-time wettings from everyone for four whole years.

In the afternoon, it began to drizzle. The Party leader disappeared and the crowd scattered. Silence fell over the entire camp except for the noisy games children played outside tent doorways, and the stones they threw at the ugly red water tanks, and the sound of them rolling in the mud and pelting each other with clods of wet dirt and insults.

As night came, the spring rain got heavier. It began to pound against the walls of our tent in a truly frightening way. But I wasn't afraid. I wasn't paying any attention, either, to Alan's moaning or to my mother's confusion or to her constant moving about the tent with some sort of purpose but without any meaning. The only thing keeping my attention was these weird changes in my body that had been going on since morning. I didn't take my eyes off my skin. I could hear it popping every time I rolled over or shifted my position on my mattress.

In less than an hour, my mother fell asleep, after my poor brother, who had been burned by hot oil that same morning, dropped off to sleep. During this hour of constant rain, my makeover into a chunk of limestone ran its course. Now I was simply a big chalk, whitish but tending toward yellow, lying on this bed. I no longer had any worries about my involuntary night-time bedwetting. After all, chalks don't pee. True, they give off dust when they are used on school chalkboards, or anywhere else, like a wall for instance, but they are completely dry. They can't pee.

My mother was sleeping quietly. I felt so sad, thinking about her. My little brother was turning over and over in bed like a pigeon being roasted on a spit. I felt sad for him, too. His burns were really bad. His hands and a large area across his chest had been seared. I knew the burn would leave him permanently disfigured, not only his skin but his spirit, too. But what was anyone supposed to do? My uncle would come back after midnight, tired out from playing so much music and singing and keeping late hours, as he always was after these evenings. He would think I was asleep. That was good. At least this night would pass well enough.

I tried to say something out loud. But no sounds came out of me.

For a chalk to make a sound, it needs fingers holding it and writing on the chalkboard or anywhere else good for writing.

'What a horrible nightmare!'

I kept trying to talk—me, this enormous column of chalk wrapped in a heavy blanket. And then, to talk to myself, but no sound came out of me this time, either. I was a chalk who was completely conscious of the strange, strange changes that had happened to it. A big chalk that would tell its painful story, later on, to a small, pale chalk, even if that chalk was lost under the feet of refugees in the camp of the Resistance.

The rain didn't stop. In fact, the sound of pounding against the sides of the tent grew louder, driven by a weirdly violent wind beating against our tent and all the others. The sound of it kept changing. At one point, it was like an endless, long wail, as if a flock of jackals had crouched all around the camp. At another moment, it was like a long and sharp whistle, as if a night watchman was calling out to suspicious people wandering the alleys of his neighbourhood. And then, pounding even more forcefully against the tent walls, it began making a sound like the big sticks that the women use on sunny days to beat the dust out of the carpets they hang on their balconies in Masakin Hanano in Aleppo.

I didn't even think about trying to go to sleep. Or I didn't have any desire to sleep. Chalk doesn't get sleepy, and I was a chalk.

The wind went on howling as it whipped around the tents while big splashes of water went on hitting the sides of the white UNICEF tents, with no let-up. Suddenly I noticed that the tent door was opening, being pushed abruptly to the inside, and that meant the sound of the pelting rain was even louder. The wind was truly frightening that night. In less than a second, the door was closed and the outside sounds dropped. I made out a shadowy shape in the doorway, inside the tent.

It's my uncle, I told myself. I hope he doesn't come over here and try to lift up my blanket. Then I shushed myself, forgetting that chalk doesn't have a voice anyway.

My uncle was holding a small lantern that gave off a pale light. I could see that he was wrapped up in a long overcoat and that he had a hood around his neck and over his head, nearly covering his face. The smell of the rain was steaming off him as he came closer. I got afraid. He would discover what was going on over here. And I couldn't predict what he would do next.

Then he was very close. He was standing at my head. He brought the lamp up level with his face and, with his free hand, he pulled the hood off his face very calmly.

'Mazyat?!' I shrieked, staring into Mazyat's full, round face which was lit up by a sad smile. And an irresistible appeal.

'Yes, it's Mazyat, my little sparrow. Don't be afraid.'

She was whispering. She set the lamp down on the tent floor and sat down beside me. I couldn't move, couldn't talk to her. I knew she wouldn't hear my voice or rather, to put it more accurately, she wouldn't hear what I was thinking. I began to feel less terrified, and what I said to myself was: I wonder what Mazyat wants? And how could she have found our tent, and where had she been during these difficult months, and why did she come now after being absent for so long?

'I came to give you some nice news. I'm not bothered about the condition you're in. I still love you, and I like you a lot better than any of the silly men that the war has turned into killers and blood merchants. On every side, I mean. In these months, I have been staying in the town of Nubbul with one of my aunts. An elderly widow who had no one to look after her. She died a few days ago, and I knew there wasn't anyone else of mine left in this whole world. The camp is the best place for widows, I told myself. Better than cities, better than towns, where all they can do is become game for the traps set by men and by the vicious fangs of rumour. And I preferred this camp to any of the others, because I found out that you were living here.'

I didn't believe what my eyes were seeing. She couldn't hear my voice, but it seemed she could read my thoughts. She could communicate with me. So, then, things would be easier than I thought? Did this mean that my mother and Alan and my uncle would understand what I was thinking, too? But what was this *nice news* that Mazyat said she had come to tell me? It had to be news about my father. A lot of people had been claiming they'd heard that he was either in Raqqa or Deir ez-Zor, or maybe even in Mosul. I was waiting for her to tell me the *nice news,* straight from her sweet mouth.

'I'm pregnant, Kamo. It's you. I'm in my fourth month.'

Mazyat undid the buttons on her wet overcoat and showed me her round belly.

What is this evening, Lord of the heavens? One nightmare right after another. What would my uncle say if he were to come in right now? How would I justify Mazyat being here—me, this piece of chalk without words? This mute?

'I'm craving chalk, my little chalk.'

Mazyat actually said this. Smiling. And then she added, 'I bought calcium pills and I've been taking them regularly. But it didn't have any effect on my cravings for chalk. I really enjoy biting into chalk, chewing it, and hearing it pop between my back teeth, *taqtaqa*. But it's my bad luck, this cursed war. The schools are all closed. If they were open, I could go into one of them and get the pupils to give me the stubs of chalk left on the board in their classroom. I could chew those instead of swallowing these miserable calcium pills.'

And then Mazyat started imitating the sound of chalk when it's crunched by teeth. *Kirrarrarraat ... kirrarrarraat.* She pulled off my covers, totally calmly. She put her hand where there used to be a space between my thighs. There was a swelling there, the shape of a piece of school chalk, and Mazyat took hold of it and picked it off. Yes, that's right, she plucked off my member which had turned into a chalk, as if she were picking a little cucumber in the field. I didn't feel any pain at all.

'I'll take it with me. No need any longer for it to stay here. I'll take a bite of it now and then to nourish the bones of your greedy son, Kamo. And then I'll come back. I will eat the rest of you. This hungry blackboard—Mazyat—will eat you up, the most delicious chalk there ever was.' Mazyat was saying these things and laughing like a tease. She gave me a rude look, pulled her hood up over her head, picked up the lantern with its pale light still flickering, and went out of the tent, though I could not see how she opened the door.

It all seemed to happen in a flash. Mazyat was suddenly not there before my eyes, as if she was an apparition or a fragment of a passing dream. All the while, the roar of the wind and the pounding of the rain outside got louder and louder.

***

After Mazyat left the tent, I couldn't sleep. It wasn't because I couldn't actually sleep, but because of my incredible transformation into a piece of chalk. I began staring into the depths of the tent, to one side and then to the other, trying to make out everything that was in here. There were the cushions my mother had piled up in one corner. Over here, I could see the photo of my father in his surgeon's dress, his fist closed around a scalpel. He was looking out at the photographer and smiling. My eyes traced the outlines of cooking pots near the gas fire. Our clothes were in a little heap under my mother's feet as she slept peacefully. When I heard her breathing, and then could hear my brother Alan's breaths mingling with hers, a powerful sense of blessedness and contentment came over me.

Finally, I saw my uncle sneaking into the tent as though he were a thief. I could see that he was gripping the bouzouki in its black leather case. He put it down quietly and carefully next to his bed. He took off his cap and his coat, which were both completely soaked from the rain, and he threw them aside without paying attention to where they landed. He got into bed and slid under the bedcovers immediately, and very soon, he was snoring. I was reassured. He wouldn't discover anything, not tonight anyway, about this thing I was going through.

It went on for hours: I went on staring into every corner of the tent as if I were discovering it for the first time. Everything looked strange to me, like it might look to a new-born baby leaving his mama's belly to come into the world. What really held my attention was that picture of my father that hung over my mother's head. Oh, Papa—if only you could know what's happening to me right now! Maybe you could do something, some operation or other, to keep this stupid comedy from happening, this change in my body.

I began thinking about my thing, which Mazyat had plucked off me. I asked myself: Was she really going to eat it? I'd heard my mother and grandmother tell stories about pregnant women who ate the ashes from cigarettes and the bits that fell off the lime wash on walls. But—a woman who ate whole pieces of chalk? I wondered what it was my mother imagined eating after she got pregnant with me.

As dawn got closer and the sound of the rain grew louder, I felt more and more uneasy. Thunder, lightning—the whole world was lit up. From inside the tent, every time the lightning flashed, it looked like a glass dome lit from above by flares. I wasn't at all frightened by any of this. Not the rumblings of the thunder nor the flashes of lightning nor this insanely heavy downpour. In any case, on that abominable night, all I could do was bow to my fate and wait for morning—which (it seemed to me through those moments) had forgotten that it was supposed to arrive.

When morning did come, I heard a lot of commotion and noise outside. My mother woke up and immediately lifted the bedcovers off my brother Alan. She made sure he was all right and then she went back to bed. But the noise outside got louder, and then it morphed into a loud stream of frightened shouts. My mother sat up in bed, the worry clear on her face. I could see she wanted to wake up her brother Ali, but she was too considerate. She knew he must be exhausted, and she didn't want to stop him from getting his sleep. So, she just stayed where she was, sitting up in bed and yawning while the terrified voices outside kept getting louder. Suddenly my uncle threw off his bedcovers and hurried over to the door to see what was going on out there.

'What's happening?' he called, standing in the doorway. 'Ya Latif ya Latif! Oh my God, the camp is flooding!' He turned around and yelled at all of us. 'Get up! Now! The water is going to get us. Layla. Kamo, Alan! Get a move on!'

My mother got out of bed, but she was at a total loss about what to do. She bent over Alan and shook him—he was still sleeping soundly—until she woke him up. My brother rubbed his eyes with his hands, which were covered in dressings, and collapsed back onto his mattress, ready to go back to sleep. My uncle shouted again.

'The camp is going under. No more sleep, Alan, get up! Kamo, wake up. Get up, help your mother and your uncle here. The waters are about to cover the whole camp.'

When he didn't get any kind of response from me, he hurried over to my bed. The moment of truth had arrived, I knew. I stayed calm. What action could I take, anyway? What choice did I have, if I didn't stay calm? A piece of chalk—and chalk doesn't sleep. Or wake up, or take any interest in rivers of water or fires. Chalk isn't scared of anyone.

My uncle bent over my mattress and shouted. 'Kamo! *Kamiiran*!' He yanked my blanket off the bed.

When he saw the state I was in, the pupils of his eyes got really wide. For quite a few seconds, he didn't speak at all. It seemed as though he had lost the ability to form words. Then he blurted out my name, in alarm mingled with astonishment: 'Kaaamiiiiraaan ...'

At that very moment, the torrent hit our tent. The water came pouring inside. My uncle left me and went toward Alan, preparing to pick him up and carry him. They hurried outside, followed by my mother, who didn't understand any of what was happening. She was so bewildered that when she saw me still lying in bed like a huge piece of chalk, she didn't take the sight of me in at all. I watched as she turned and hurried after my uncle without even glancing back. As if she hadn't even recognized me.

So, there I was, alone in my bed. I didn't know how I was supposed to get up. I no longer had two feet, or any hands, or a pair of wings, of course. I was just a solid white pillar lying there absolutely still. I needed someone to roll me or push me along in front of them, or to pick me up and sling me over one shoulder.

I stared at the photograph of my father hanging on the wall over my mother's bed. My father, wearing his surgical dress. He was looking at me, and I thought I saw an expression of discomfort and dismay on his face. I imagined him suddenly moving. Coming out of the photo and coming over in order to help me.

My father walked out of the photo.

The level of the water inside the tent rose. I began to feel it—to feel wet. I heard people screaming, women wailing, children crying.

'All hell's breaking loose. It's my fault, Kamo.' I was hearing a voice I knew. A sweet voice I had lost a few years ago. 'How many of these hells am I going to see?' I asked myself.

Outside, it really did seem to be like hell on earth, or the end of the world. I could see the shapes of men and women being submerged in water, still carrying their most important belongings on their heads along with their children. I saw men from the Red Crescent running from one tent to another, trying to rescue children and old people. I could also see the traces of shit that the Party hack had strewn all around as he gave his speech. The flowing water was carrying the shit away from the drowning camp.

'Kamo, come on! Follow me.'

It was the same sweet voice, ordering me to move. I knew that voice. It belonged to my father. My father who, a few moments before, I had imagined walking out of his photograph. I answered him, even though I couldn't see him anywhere. I couldn't keep the despair out of my voice.

'Papa, I don't have any feet. I can't escape. It's a terrible ordeal, this state that I'm in.'

'The flood is your crutch, boy. Lean on the floodwaters.'

Before I could answer, the rushing water swept over me. At first, I managed to float on its surface. I was turning over, though, and swinging, and bobbing, and I collided into some pieces of wood and other objects that were also floating along on the surface. There seemed to be thousands of broken olive branches that the angry stream of water had stripped off and dragged along with it. I kept on disappearing beneath the surface and then bobbing up again, floating along and bumping into more things that the torrent of water had plundered from the tents of all these evacuees.

I had no idea where my mother and brother and uncle had gone. They had disappeared. I was amazed that they had deserted me without showing any concern about what would happen to me. I didn't really care what happened to them, either. I was completely occupied with myself and everything that was happening to me right now. It distracted me from thinking about them at all.

I went on floating and spinning, going underwater and popping up, sinking again and then breaking the surface. The sight of the olive branches floating on top of the rushing water made a fine picture. As far as I could see, the water's surface was overlaid by olive branches that caromed into one another and got tangled up together. I wanted to get close enough to one of these olive branches to get its sympathy and consolation, since I felt so alone out here, but instead I collided suddenly with some piled-up shit bobbing along on the water around me, an unbelievable amount of it.

'Where is all this shit coming from? This shit that's besieging Zaytun Kurd Dagh. From where?'

'Shit has filled the whole country. Don't pay any attention to it. Keep going, Kamo. Give yourself up to the water.' It was my father's sweet, kind voice again.

The flood swept me far away from the camp. I could feel myself melting in the water. 'I'm made of calcium,' I found myself saying. 'And calcium breaks up fast when it's dunked in water. I'm a piece of chalk being carried away by the flood. That means I'll dissolve. The end is near.'

I thought about this. My end. I sensed I was losing large parts of my body. No one was going to rescue me. I was alone in this trial, completely alone. I had got a lot weaker since the rushing water had begun carrying me away from the tent—several kilometres, by now. I was very thin and a lot smaller than I had been.

'I'm a long way away from the camp. I've gone along with the currents, I didn't resist. It's impossible to go back, and rescue is impossible, too. What's not impossible is that I'm dissolving slowly into this moving stream of water. That is—what's not impossible is death. That's the only thing that isn't impossible. So, it's the end.'

‘The end is just a tall tale, Kamo. That’s all it is, son. A legend. There are no ends. Don’t they say: Such-and-such a war has ended? But it’s all relative, since wars don’t end, and they won’t end. Death, too, and massacres. The evil of human beings. This circle, which has no beginning. Existence, I mean. Do you believe that existence will end? No, never. There’s no extinction, no utter end to being.’

‘How can that be, Papa?’

‘Because existence, because being here on this earth, is a circle. Every part of it goes round and round. Time, movement, place, matter. Matter is nothing more than a circle, beginning with the atom and going all the way to the endless universe. Rings within rings. So, don’t you allow yourself to believe in anything that’s labelled *end*. Or *non-existence*.’

I didn’t understand my father’s words, which did not seem to have a clear meaning. I was melting. I was disappearing. Soon, I wouldn’t exist. I was vanishing completely, so how could my father claim that there was no such thing as non-existence? What was it, if it wasn’t a big piece of chalk dissolving in floodwaters? And then, this surging stream of water carrying me would mingle with all the rivers that went on and on out here.

I am disappearing into nothing. This is the only thing that’s real now, the only thing I’m living, Father. It is my end. The end of me. The end of my story.

October 2018 – January 2019

Author's acknowledgment

My gratitude goes to all who have provided information that benefited me in writing this novel, especially my friend Engineer Salah Hanan of Afrin.

Translator's note

Names of places and people have been spelled as they would be transliterated from Arabic (rather than Kurdish). When there exists a familiar Arabic equivalent, that is used (Aleppo rather than Halab).

While the Arabic text states that Layla Aghazadeh was a student and teacher of English, in the companion novel *A Green Bus Leaves Aleppo,* she is an Arabic teacher, and so we have made this change to preserve consistency between the two novels.

What are known as YPG (Yekîneyên Parastina Gel, or People's Defence/ Protection Units) in English are rendered here as People's Defence Units, the armed wing of the major Syrian Kurdish Party, the PYD, incorporating both police functions (Protection Units) and military action (Defence Units).

Jan Dost

Author

Jan Dost, born in 1966, is a native of Kobani in the Aleppo region of Syria. A student of natural sciences at the University of Aleppo (1985-89), he embarked on a career in journalism in the roles of reporter and editor, currently for the *Kurdistan Chronicle* (published in English in Erbil, Iraq) He is editor-in-chief of the Arabic-language magazine *Kurdistan*.

Jan Dost has published five novels in Kurdish and eleven in Arabic (as well as four volumes of poetry). Translations of his fiction have appeared in Spanish, Turkish, Arabic, Kurdish, Polish, Persian, and Italian. Almost all of his Arabic novels have appeared in Kurdish and vice versa. His Kurdish novel *Mirnâme* (2008), for instance, appeared in Turkish, and Persian; the Arabic novel *'Ashiq al-mutarjim* (2013) has appeared in Italian, Kurdish, and Turkish; the Arabic novel *Bas akhdar yughadir Halab* (2019) has been translated into Spanish and Kurdish. Safe Corridor is his first novel to appear in English.

Jan Dost has received numerous awards: in Syria (Short Story Prize, 1992); in the Kurdistan Region of Iraq (Hussein Arif Award for Creativity, 2014; Mem u Zin Literature Festival Award, 2021); in Germany (Kurdish Poetry Prize, 2012); and in Austria (Sharafnama Award for Kurdish Culture, 2021). He has also translated literary works from Kurdish and Persian into Arabic, and from Arabic into Kurdish, and has participated in translation workshops as well as speaking at conferences and book fairs. Since 2000, Jan Dost has resided in Germany and is a German citizen. His most recent work in Arabic is *al-Asir al-faransawi* (2022).

Marilyn Booth

Translator

Marilyn Booth is professor emerita, Faculty of Asian and Middle Eastern Studies and Magdalen College, Oxford University. At Oxford, she held the endowed Khalid bin Abdallah Al Saud Professorship for the Study of the Contemporary Arab World, 2015-23; at Edinburgh, she held the Iraq Chair in Arabic and Islamic Studies, 2009-15. Her research publications focus on Arabophone women's writing and the ideology of gender debates in the nineteenth century, most recently *The Career and Communities of Zaynab Fawwaz: Feminist Thinking* in Fin-de-siècle *Egypt* (Oxford University Press, 2021). She has in recent years been a research fellow at the Institute for Advanced Study, Princeton; l'Institut d'études avancées, Paris; Neubauer Collegium for Society and Culture, University of Chicago; and visiting professor, l'EHESS, in addition to numerous earlier research fellowships.

Safe Corridor is the twenty-first volume of Arabic fiction that Booth has rendered into English. Other recent translations include Omani author Zahran Alqasmi's *Honey Hunger*; Omani author Jokha Alharthi's *Silken Gazelles*; and Lebanese author Hoda Barakat's *Voices of the Lost*. Her translation of Alharthi's *Celestial Bodies* won the 2019 Man Booker International Prize. In addition to other novels by Alharthi and Barakat, her translations include novels by Hassan Daoud, Elias Khoury, Alia Mamdouh, Hamdi Abu Golayyel, Latifa al-Zayyat, Somaya Ramadan, and others, as well as a memoir by Nawal al-Saadawi and three short story collections. Her first venture into translating nineteenth-century fiction, Alis al-Bustani's 1891 novel *Sa'iba* is forthcoming with Oxford World's Classics.